The Skry Pit Kids

By Jacqueline Bellew

Illustrated by Dan McCloskey
Edited by Sarah Mann

An environmentally friendly book printed and bound in England by
www.printondemand-worldwide.com

Mixed Sources
Product group from well-managed forests, and other controlled sources
FSC www.fsc.org Cert no. TT-COC-002641
© 1996 Forest Stewardship Council

PEFC Certified
This product is from sustainably managed forests and controlled sources
PEFC PEFC/16-33-415
www.pefc.org

This book is made entirely of chain-of-custody materials

FastPrint Publishing

www.fast-print.net/store.php

THE SKRY PIT KIDS

All characters are fictional.
Any similarity to any actual person is purely coincidental.

A catalogue record for this book is available from the British Library

ISBN 978-178035-659-4

First published 2013 by
FASTPRINT PUBLISHING
Peterborough, England.

Potosí, Bolivia – thirteen-year-old Agustin Leandro works in the Rich Mountain mine, one of the most dangerous mines in the world. He and his brothers live in a shack outside the mine entrance; he has worked there since the age of nine, earning less than £1.50 or $3 a day.

Today there are over 115 million children working in dangerous conditions worldwide. Many are less than ten years old. – Source: UNICEF

This book is dedicated to children past and present whose childhoods have been lost to poverty and the greed of others.

'Overcoming poverty is not a task of charity, it is an act of justice'- Nelson Mandela

Synopsis

Working down the mine was Tim's worst nightmare but making friends with Jonnie and Evie made him think that maybe working down the deepest, most dangerous pit in England wouldn't be half as bad as the dream he'd had last night. After all, if his brother and sister had done it for this long surely it couldn't be that bad?

But Jonnie isn't who they think he is and when the children are forced to flee the mine, their village and families, the dark curse of Skry seems to follow them.

The Skry Pit Kids is a children's historical fiction aimed at age 9-11. It tells the story of five children as they go to work down the most dangerous mine in England. Set in 1839, just before The Children's Act forbade children under 13 to work for 12 hours a day in the dark, it tells the story of the children's first terrible day down the pit and the disaster that forces them to run for their lives.

Reviews:

Brilliant book really feels like you are there in the mines with the characters doing what they are doing with them. I would not like to live down the mines because it is dirty and cold and you would have a very easy chance of dying.

Lois Xeros aged 9 - Tyne and Wear.

I have been down a mine and this book is very realistic. It feels like you are down the mine! I wouldn't want to work there like Tim and Jonnie because of the dusty smokey air. I would like a dog like Beamer!

Leon aged 12 - Tyne and Wear.

I think that Annie is sad, but then she is probably bad! But not all bad...

Laura aged 10 - Bedfordshire.

About the Author

The Skry Pit Kids is the first in a series of 3 books by Jacqueline Bellew. The books are the result of 10 years of research into mining. The author is a writer, researcher and lecturer and a member of the Society of Authors. She lives in Bedford with her husband and has 3 boys, 3 cats and 3 chickens. You can find more information on the book at: www.theskrypitkids.co.uk.

Follow us on Facebook: https://www.facebook.com/skrypitkids

Or Twitter@ theskrypitkids

About the Illustrator

Dan McCloskey

Dan McCloskey is originally from Ireland. He loves stories. When he is not illustrating he is working on animations and cartoons. He lives in the North of England in Sunderland.

Acknowledgments

I would like to thank a number of people without whom this book would never have been written. To my illustrator Dan whose wonderful drawings help bring my characters to life. To Sarah my editor whose eagle eye for detail and lexical expertise was invaluable in combing through the story for any historical inconsistencies. To the many miners, historians and people with an interest in mining that have shared their knowledge and enthusiasm for the project.

I would also like to thank my family, Robert, Alex, Harry and William and my mother, Kate, who have lived with the kids through bad times and good. To my sister Pam, her partner, Pete, and their children Sophie, Lois and Leon and their friends, who reviewed the book in its early stages. Particular thanks go to Lois and Leon Xeros who sat with me in the pitch dark Skinningrove mine so that we could really imagine what it felt like for Tim, Jonnie, Daisy, Jo and Evie to work for 13 hours with not even a chink of light (we only sat there for 15 minutes and that was bad enough!).

And finally last but not least thanks to my father, Don Baxter, whose obsession with the history of mining started me off on this adventure.

'Why must I sit behind the door

So many hours away from you,

And hear the putters shout and roar

And naught but shut and open do?'

- The Trapper's Petition

(from *The Pit Children* by Eric Forster)

Chapter 1

It was black, pitch black, blacker than anything he'd ever known. All around him there were groans and creaks, noises coming out of the inky blackness. He tried to stand up but barely got half way before his head hit hard on cold rock. He felt for the base of the door; maybe, if he crouched very low in the corner, the Pit Wife wouldn't find him. The groaning became louder and the ground below him trembled. Somewhere, somewhere near him, the terrible screaming began. He tried to get his breath, but the heat and dust choked him. He reached for his kerchief, desperately trying to block the stench of the poisonous gases that were filling his lungs, cutting off the last remnants of clean air.

Suddenly the trap door dividing him from the rest of the narrow pit passage sprang open and something began to crawl out of the tunnel towards him. "Dad, Dad, help us, Dad," cried Tim, sobbing as he struggled desperately to close the door, pushing hard on the soaking wood, his feet slipping in the black mud. Almost there, Tim gave one last enormous heave and the door crashed shut, in front of him.

Sobbing with relief, he leaned back against the blackened walls, blood pouring from a cut in his hands. From behind the door he could hear something shuffling around in the dark. Turning away from the door, Tim lit the last remnants of his candle, illuminating the dark passage behind him. As he raised the tiny stub, the sight in front of him was terrible: rocks and rubble blocked the passageway and just in front of him a dead rat lay crushed under a heavy coal wagon, its head lolling limply to one side. Seized with panic, Tim crawled towards it and, with the last of his strength, peered into the wagon. The stench was terrible now; a mixture of burning and rotten eggs. Blinded by the smoke Tim could just make out a dark shape moving inside the coal wagon.

"Daisy, is that you Daisy?" he croaked. Raising the candle, Tim peered inside and gasped with horror as a voice echoed through the darkness: "It's me, Timmy, it's your Daisy. I remembered you, Timmy – I've come to take you home."

"No I am NOT your Daisy," shouted an indignant voice. "I shove harder than any girl and when I get back in that bed, that's what you'll be getting." Tim looked in the direction of the voice, and there, sat on the floor was Jo, rubbing his backside and groaning.

"These nightmares are getting beyond the pale; sooner you get down that pit for real the better it'll be for us that have to share a bed with you," grumbled the skinny lad in the nightshirt.

A loud banging on the window made them both jump.

"Three o'clock and ready for work," shouted the voice. "Stir yourselves, bonny lads and lasses."

The knocking at the window grew more insistent, as Dave the Knocker Man waited to see some sign of life before he moved on to wake the occupants of the next house. "Come on you lot, shake a leg; I've got another thirty houses to knock up yet," he shouted up at the window.

"All right, all right, Dave, keep your hair on man," they heard their father shout, from downstairs.

Tim's little sisters, five-year-old Lottie, and four-year-old Mary, were still asleep in the bed next to him, and he could just make out the shapes of his six-year-old twin brothers, Jack and Den, hiding under the covers next to him, while the two older children pulled on their clothes, shivering in the darkness of the morning.

"Come on birthday boy, hurry about it, big day today, working lad." Jo grinned at his little brother, pulling the covers off him and giving him a friendly slap.

"You'll have to be sharper than this when you're opening the traps or you'll be for it," said Daisy with a frown.

Jo shrugged and raised his eyebrows at Tim. "Hark at her, the expert," retorted Jo. "Boss of the mine she is now, you know."

Daisy glared at Jo and handed Tim a small package. "Here you go lad. Happy birthday, big man!" she said with a little smile.

Tim took the package, touched that his big sister had remembered. "Can I open it now?" he asked with a grin.

"No pet, keep it for later. It's something for you when you get down the pit," she replied.

Tim carefully placed the tiny package, wrapped in brown paper, on the table beside the bed, bracing himself to face the cold. Although the days were beginning to get warmer, the biting cold of the dark morning reminded them that winter wasn't quite over yet. His bare feet hit the icy floorboards and he quickly reached for his woollen trousers and shift. Pulling them on, he made his way down the steep wooden stairs that led to the front room. His dad, Jay, was already up and slurping a big mug of thick tea at the kitchen table. As Tim appeared, he handed him a big mug full of the tea.

"Happy birthday, son," smiled Jay. "Not every day you have a birthday and start work for the first time," he said, giving Tim a playful dig in the ribs. "Looking forward to it?"

Tim tried to smile. A birthday was a big thing for a lad and normally he'd be jumping about with excitement by now. But today was different: today he'd leave the sunshine and fresh air to spend twelve hours down the deepest, most dangerous mine in the land. Today was his first day down the black hole they called the Skry Pit. He'd known for years that this day would come eventually, that the family needed the money he'd bring in. But the dream kept on coming back to haunt him. That same dream, over and over again, night after night, leaving him panting and sweating in fear. He didn't dare tell his mum; she'd think it was a bad omen. She believed in things like that, and there was no way he wanted to pile more worry onto her shoulders.

"Of course, I'm really looking forward to going to work with you and our kid[1]," he nodded, looking over at Jo. "I'll be a real working man at last!"

Jo shook his head, muttering, "You might not be saying that after you've been down there for a bit."

"You'll be fine, our kid," his mum interjected quickly, putting down a big jug of porridge and milk in front of them. Stealing a nervous glance at her husband, she continued. "You're a big lad now, and there'll be a surprise for you when you get home tonight."

Jay's expression suddenly darkened as he turned to his eldest son. "You don't want to be picking up any bad habits from our Jo," he said, slapping Tim on the shoulder. "You'll go to work like a real man. No whingeing and whining and wanting to go stopping at home with mam and the bairns." Tim glanced quickly at Jo; he hated it when his dad got at his elder brother, but everybody knew that Jo hated going down the pit. He was always skiving off with one of his heads, as he called them. Everyone knew it was just so he could stay at home with Mam.

Jo looked dejected and turned away from Tim. He'd find out soon enough, he'd soon learn what being 'a real man' was all about.

---

[1] Northern term meaning brother, sister or child.

Tim tried to look pleased, but his stomach was turning over at the thought of what the day held in store. It would be a long time before he would be able to come home and enjoy whatever birthday surprise his mam had planned for him. Twelve whole hours in the pitch black, sat there all alone. Jay tore off a corner of the thick slice of bread and dripping that was his special treat for being the man of the house. "Here, this'll set you up right." The rich salty taste hit Tim's taste buds and he savoured the moment, the rest of them looking on in envy as they ploughed their way through their thick porridge. It was a long walk to the mine and they'd need it to set them up for the day.

As the clock struck half past three, Jay took a last slurp, gave a sigh and rose heavily from the table. Moving towards the door, he took up his old coat and lunch bait, and put it in the tin that was slung around his belt. They would all eat the same that lunchtime: thick slices of bread with Mam's strawberry jam in it. Smiling for a moment, Tim let himself remember last summer, picking strawberries then lying back on the warm grass feeling the sun on his face. There'd be none of that this year; he would spend his days, the rest of his days in the darkness, until his lungs gave out and he was an old man. One week a year holiday if he was lucky.

Jessie glanced nervously at him. She knew exactly what was going through his mind, but there was nothing she could do about it; that was his lot and he'd just have to accept it, like they all did.

"It's thirsty work down the mine so here you go." Handing them all two tin bottles of water, she stood by the door, giving each one a hug as they made their way out into the dark cobbled street. As Tim passed her she held out a stub of candle.

"Here lad, here's your pit rat; you'll have to make this last. Don't have it lit all the time, just when you need to. You'll not get another." Tim held out his hand taking the tiny stub of candle that didn't look as if it would last more than half an hour; as he took it, Mam leaned forward and gave him a big hug. "You'll be all right, bonny lad, you're a big strong one now. It's our Daisy that's worrying us, I just don't know if she's got it in her to be a hurrier," she sighed.

"She'll be all right, Mam," said Tim, trying to make her feel better. "Daisy is a tough old bird and she's done well as a trappy lass."

"Aye, maybe so," replied Jessie, biting her lip; "But I remember when our Jo came home from his first day as a hurrier; he was that bad, all bleeding and sore, and his poor little head, I had to put a compress on it all night. He didn't want to go back the next day but we made him and he was crying all the while. I don't know how our Daisy will get on down there, she's not over-strong and pulling those heavy coal wagons isn't fit work for a lass." Mam's face creased with worry as she looked down the street in the direction of the mine. They all knew that there was no choice for Daisy, with seven kids in the family and another on the way; they all had to do what they could to bring in a wage.

"Howay Jessie, let the lad go and stop mothering him," said Jay, giving his wife a sharp pat, his face creased with irritation. They all had to get on with it and it didn't help when Jessie went all motherly on them.

Giving a little shiver, Mam turned to Tim; Jay could be hard when he wanted to. Yes, he had a soft side, but it was only really her that ever saw it. And Daisy, of course – Daisy could do no wrong in her father's eyes.

Turning to Tim she forced herself to smile. "Anyway pet, you never mind me. It'll be all right, you'll see. I'll have you a nice dinner ready when you get home, nice bit of meat and some tatties[2] for your birthday." Tim smiled bravely in return; he'd do anything to make her proud of him.

"Don't worry Mam, I'll be all right," he said, patting her comfortingly as he moved past her into the dark cobbled street.

---

[2] Slang for potatoes

"Don't forget this, bonny lad," said a squeaky voice, and Tim looked behind him to see his six-year-old brother holding out the parcel that Daisy had given him earlier.

"Ta, mate," he said, ruffling the little lad's hair. "See ya marrer." The younger boy beamed with delight. He worshipped Tim, always had done. Tim gulped back a tear; his little brother Jack wasn't really like other kids, he wouldn't understand that Tim was going to be away for so long.

Den, Jack's twin, had understood right enough: "Off toothpit," he'd said, smiling all over his chubby face, as he still lay cosily in bed beside his younger sisters. "Off to-the-pit." But Jack wasn't like other lads; he'd been all right until he was one, then his mam started to worry that he wasn't growing like the others. When Jack still wasn't talking by his third birthday, it was clear that there was something badly wrong with him and, as the years went by, and Den started to do the things the other boys did – climbing, getting into trouble, scrumping apples – it was clear to everyone that Jack would never be quite like other children. But he seemed happy enough, spending hours playing with the sticks and stones he collected from the fields, arranging them into patterns on the ground.

Tim tried to put them both out of his mind; he needed all his wits about him for what lay ahead. Turning towards the lane, he paused for a minute; it was still too dark to see beyond the lane but already he could sense it brooding in the darkness: Skry Pit, waiting to swallow him up.

The village of Skry was transforming now as lines of men, women and children took to the cobbled streets, leaving their cottages and making for the dirt road that led to the pit. It was a good two miles' walking before they would arrive at the yawning entrance hole and many of them looked half asleep. Some of the fathers were carrying sleeping children on their backs, their thumbs in their mouths as they slumbered on. Tim started in surprise as Daisy and Jo pushed past him, jostling for position amongst a noisy group just in front of them. Daisy was thirteen and had worked down the mine since she was nine but, as Mam had said, it would be a big change for her today, too: she was changing jobs from being a trapper, opening and shutting the doors in the mine, to the much harder job of being a hurrier, pulling the corves or coal trucks, loaded with coal, from the coal face to the end of the seam.

Daisy's round face beamed at the thought of her new job. Her dark hair was smooth and silky and tied at the back by a pretty green ribbon that Mam had bought for her at the fair, and her dimpled cheeks and ready smile gave her a friendly look that made her very popular with the other children. She loved to talk too, a trait that didn't make her too popular with Mrs Thundertone, the Sunday school teacher. Only last week she'd been put into the corner with the dunce's cap on, for talking to Susie Briar during one of Mrs Thundertone's never-ending talks about SIN and what terrible things would happen if you did a SIN, one of the strict Sunday school teacher's favourite subjects.

Now she hopped and skipped around the little group, thrilled at the thought that her new job would earn her more money than the other children: that she could lord it over the younger trappy lads and lasses.

"I'll be waving to the lot of you, stuck in one place, sitting beside your little doors while I'm off doing a proper job."

Tim could tell what she was thinking: that she'd make Dad proud of her, that she wouldn't be like Jo, coming home whingeing and crying. She loved to think of herself as top dog in the family, and today she was in her element.

"It's just not that easy, our Daisy," said Jo, shaking his head like a wise old man. "They're really heavy, them corves, and you have to move quick you know, or they'll beat you. Some of them slopes are the very devil to climb and your knees'll be bleeding before you know it."

"You always think you can do everything better than me. Well, you'll find out the hard way." He was bolder now he was out of Dad's earshot. Maybe now he'd be able to talk some sense into the girl. At thirteen he'd already been working as a hurrier for a year: the muscles on his chest, and tell-tale bald spot on his head caused by pushing the heavy loads of coal, marked him out as experienced. He rubbed the red angry bald spot. His heads, as he called them, were getting worse. Dad thought it was just an excuse to stay at home, away from the hated pit, but the mild headaches that had started when he began as a hurrier had become steadily worse. Sometimes he saw flashing lights and smelled strange smells just before the pain began, and once it began it was impossible for him to push a loaded corve with his head. He hated Dad thinking he was soft, that he wasn't hard enough to be proud of. Mam understood and did what she could to defend him when Jay lost his temper. But it didn't stop his dad from thinking badly of him, or Daisy for thinking she was more of a man than he was, he thought ruefully, shaking his head.

A lot of the children in the group were still trappy lads and lasses, sitting each day for twelve or thirteen hours in the pitch darkness in the dark passageways of the mine. Many of the younger ones were the ones Tim had seen being carried on their dads' shoulders. Tim had heard tales about what happened when they arrived; about how the little ones screamed and cried when they were left alone in the darkness. About how they were beaten if they fell asleep and didn't open the trap doors when they were asked. He knew that he was lucky that he'd been able to get to the grand old age of nine without having to work there.

His feet were hurting already. The boots that Mam had looked out for him had been worn by six other lads before they passed to him. He wasn't used to the heavy wooden soles, which dragged on the polished cobbles and made his legs feel like lead.

As the group reached the end of the village and headed out across the fields, Tim fell into step with his dad and another man.

"You heard about Pigstone Pit then, Paddy," said his dad, shaking his head sadly.

"Aye, our Jenny told us about it last night; she'd been over to the town collecting washing from the big house and the women did nothing but talk about it," the man said, with a heavy sigh. "Biggest blast for a while, blew the whole of the main passage way and the whole of the shaft, folk couldn't get in or out. They say the fire lasted two days before they could get enough water up to flood the thing and put it out. And old Ma Nicholson, a nasty business and no mistake." Paddy shook his head solemnly.

"I heard she lost her lads down there," Jay said, sadly.

"Aye, but that was only the half of it," the other man continued, heavily. "It weren't just Jimmy and Simon she lost, though that would have been bad enough. No, she lost her little lad Mark and all; four years old he was, and only his second day in the pit."

Tim's heart missed a beat. He wanted to block his ears, not to listen to any more, but he couldn't help himself.

"Aye, and her girl Nellie, and she was only eight," he went on.

"My Jenny was talking to a woman who'd been there, at the pit head with Ma Nicholson. She said that one by one they brought them up, all wrapped in sheets. But it didn't hide much," he added in a hushed whisper. "You could see how bad they were, from the blood and all, and the terrible smell of burning."

Tim's stomach lurched. He couldn't let the men see him like this; with a single leap he managed to make it into a nearby ditch before the remains of his breakfast re-appeared. The sweat poured down his neck and all he could think of was the dream. The two men carried on talking, so caught up in the bad news that they didn't notice that Tim had disappeared into the ditch.

"Aye, but that still weren't the worst of it. It was what happened when they took what was left of poor little Nellie back to her house. They found her mam next morning, sitting beside the coffin, lost her mind they say."

Tim felt hot tears begin. But he couldn't cry now: if he cried they'd see, they'd think he was like Jo; soft, not much of a man. But the feelings were strong, too strong to ignore. He couldn't go on, he couldn't do it; face the heat, the dirt, the stench, and worse: the creature that crept out of his dream, the creature that waited for him down Skry Pit.

Chapter 2

Jo was hot and upset, his head was already hurting him and the scabs on his knees caused by crawling along the rough stone tunnels for twelve hours a day were starting to bleed. Although his sister drove him mad most of the time, deep down he was very fond of her. The thought of her having to do the job that he hated was really upsetting him. Catching up with her again, he had one last go at trying to let her know what she was really in for.

"It's not like you think it's going to be, it's hard, our Daisy, really hard, and there's not much time for standing chatting. You'll be laughing on the other side of your face when your bonny hair starts to fall out, and you get a baldy like mine." He pointed to the bald spot which looked swollen, red and angry. Daisy, unimpressed, speeded up, overtaking him, nose in the air, trying to ignore what he said. "I remember my first day as a hurrier, I was that tired I couldn't even eat me dinner. And me legs were that sore and bleeding, Mam had to wash them all down when I got home." Jo went on, jumping ahead of her, his normally placid face twisted with concern.

"Aye, well, that's you, isn't it, Jo, always moaning and groaning, always making Mam feel sorry for you," Daisy retorted, her face wrinkled with disgust. "Dad always said that I was more of a man than you," she shouted, her hands on her hips.

Jo turned away, shaking his head in despair. She'd learn the hard way, Daisy always did. She'd never listen to anyone else; she always thought she knew best. She was much closer to their dad than he was; Jay always had a smile for Daisy. His 'Little man', he called her. Jo was closer to his mam. They were both quiet and softly spoken, both liked nature and animals. Sometimes, when he was off work with one of his headaches, she'd take him across the fields and show him all the different insects and birds in the fields around the village. She'd show him how to carefully scrape the outlines of the birds onto a slate. She knew the names of them all, even though she couldn't read and write. He loved that time with her, with the young ones being looked after by Mrs Starwort down the lane. He revelled in the unaccustomed luxury of having her to himself, even if it was for a short time.

"It's easy being a hurrier, all you have to do is hurry your big bottom through those doors. Aye, and it's a big bot and all, ye'll not get that though them tiny doors in a hurry. It'll get stuck there and you'll be having to wait for the next corve to push you through. You'll be like a cork, bang you'll go, kerrrr pop!" laughed a tiny blond boy, loving the attention he was getting from a group of children who giggled slyly at the thought of the regal Daisy popping out of a passageway like a cork out of a bottle; that would sort her bossiness out for a while. Daisy turned to him, cuffing him none too gently across the backside.

"You watch your lip and don't you dare cheek your betters: your mam'll be furious when she hears you've said that B word, Peter Smythe – and I'll tell of you, mark me if I don't," said Daisy, looking every inch the school teacher. "And worse by far, I'll tell Mrs Thundertone of you and then you'll be sorry."

Young Smythe paled at the thought, thinking of their Sunday school teacher and the strap that she kept behind the door, especially made for bad lads like him that cheeked their betters.

Jo shook his head. Daisy could always make the younger ones behave – she would have made a fine Sunday school teacher if she hadn't needed to go down the pit, he thought ruefully. None of the children had the chance to go to any sort of school apart from Sunday school. There wasn't time; they were either out working at the pit, or helping out with the younger ones. They also had to help out in the garden, tending the half dozen chickens or helping to plant and harvest their few vegetables – potatoes, leeks and, if they were lucky, a few nice carrots to put in a stew and stave off the hunger that seemed to be with them nearly all of the time.

* * *

Tim crawled out from the ditch; the sickness had passed now but Dad and Paddy were some way ahead. In the pale grey light of the morning he could just about make out their tall figures, still engrossed in tales of pit disasters. Behind him, in the distance, thin wisps of smoke from the village curled up into the dawn; in front of him, the mine workings were just visible over the blood-red horizon. He couldn't do it, he knew he couldn't go down there; he'd rather face any amount of hidings from his dad than the creature from his dreams. His mind made up, he turned back towards the village and slowly began the journey home.

* * *

"Not thinking of going anywhere are you, Carter?"

Tim looked round and his heart sank; Annie Giles smirked at him from the side of the road.

"It's no business of yours, Giles," retorted Tim.

"You Carters are all the same; you lot with your mad brother and that stupid wimp Jo; him that's always crying all the time." She sniggered, her eyes slyly eyeing up his bait tin. "Aye, and awful Daisy, mincing about with her tatty ribbon, thinking she's a cut above. You'll both be crying when the Pit Wife comes for you."

Tim blanched. Everyone had heard of the Pit Wife, the ghost of a mining woman who had been killed there years ago. They said that if you went down into the deepest part of the mine, that you could hear her groaning and moaning, looking for a way out. There were passages in the mine that not even the oldest, most experienced miners would go, for fear that the Pit Wife would get them.

"You shut your gob, Giles, or you'll get what's coming to you," Tim shouted bravely, desperately hoping that Geordie, Annie's big brother, wasn't anywhere near to hear him. Not that Annie wasn't bad enough on her own. After all, he'd seen her beat up lads far bigger than him. But this morning the fear of Annie seemed like nothing in comparison to his fear of the mine.

Annie came towards him, her fist bared. "What did you say, Carter?"

Tim turned to her, ready to defend himself, when suddenly a dark shadow fell between them. A hand grabbed him by the scruff of the neck, lifting him into the air. He choked as the hand squeezed the life out of him and Geordie Giles's hot stinking breath filled his nostrils.

"Wotcha, mate," said the bigger boy with a grin, his face level with Tim's. "I think me and me sister here need to give you a little lesson in manners now. I'll have that parcel off you for starters," said Geordie Giles, grabbing the present out of Tim's hand.

Tim wriggled like a worm on a hook. "Give us it back, that's mine," he cried, hot tears of anger beginning to run down his cheeks.

"Aw look at old wimpy bottom here, bubbling like a babby," Geordie Giles laughed.

Suddenly the thought of the horrible pair getting their hands on the present, that Daisy had saved for months to buy, was too much for Tim and, mustering all of his strength, he smashed his fist hard into Giles's meaty shoulder.

Dropping Tim with a cry, Geordie Giles sank to the ground, still clutching the tiny package, but at least letting go of the precious bait. Tim lunged for it, grasping the tin in both hands. Giles roared and made another grab for him, but Tim was faster and, turning tail, he began to run, back in the direction of the pit. It wasn't long before he caught sight of Paddy and his dad at the top of the bank and, running up the steep hill once again, he fell into step beside his father.

"Well lad, you ready for this?" said Jay gruffly, seeming hardly to notice that Tim was panting like a dog.

Tim's dad regarded him with solemn eyes. Jay was a huge man who looked much older than his forty years. He coughed all the time, often keeping them all awake at night. He did have a soft side, but didn't show it very often. He could be especially gruff when he was upset, as he was today: he hated sending his kids down the mine, but there was no choice. He earned a good wage down there but it still wasn't enough to keep the family. Since Tim's mam had to give up working when she became pregnant again, they had known that it would only be a matter of time before Tim would have to work alongside Jo and Daisy. He and Jessie desperately hoped that Tim would be a bit braver than Jo.

"I'm fine, Dad," replied Tim, desperately trying to keep up with his dad's long strides.

"You know what you've got to do, then?"

"Yes, Dad, Daisy's told me."

Daisy had told him all right; she took real pleasure in terrifying him with terrible stories of dead boys, and ghosts that lived down the old mine. He remembered the last time that Daisy had decided to tell him a few stories of what it was like down the pit. It was last Sunday afternoon and a big group of them all gathered together after Sunday school. They wandered around the village for a while, getting bored, and finally made their way down to the cave near the sea. The long two-mile walk from Skry village was well worth it, for a couple of hours of freedom away from the chores they all had to do around the house. The cave was at the far end of what they called the West Beach. It was only accessible at low tide, and even then it was quite difficult to get to. Only the children were normally brave enough to make the climb and that was exactly what made it an ideal place to get away from the grown-ups. Often big groups of them would gather in the cave, lighting fires and eating food that they'd managed to sneak out of the house.

That day, Daisy was in her element. The children had lit a fire in the cave and there must have been about fifteen of them huddled around it. They were all from the village and most of them either already worked down the mine or would be starting there some time soon.

"The Pit Wife goes after the new ones," Daisy said, her eyes lighting up. "She likes young lads and lasses 'cos they scare easy. Little Timmy Johnson had only been working down the mine for a couple of weeks; he was only eight and really scared at the thought of going down there and sitting all alone in the dark …."

Tim turned his face to the wall, hoping that no one could see his expression. She was going to say something horrible, he knew it.

Daisy continued: "Well, so, there was little Timmy sitting in the darkness, waiting for someone to come along and tell him it was time to go home." Daisy threw a sly glance in Tim's direction.

"But everyone else had gone," she announced with a flourish. "They'd forgotten about him and left him there alone, totally alone; a small boy, away from his mother for the first time; alone and afraid in the deepest darkest part of the mine: the part, it was said, that was haunted by the terrible ghost of the Pit Wife. Course he didn't know that, 'cos he didn't know what time it was, so he just sat there: poor little Timmy." She turned away with a little giggle.

Tim's face creased with annoyance; she would, she would go and call the boy Timmy – that was just about the last straw. Looking desperately towards the light at the entrance to the cave, he wondered if there was any way he could make a break for it. But a quick glance back at the children told him it was no good; some of them were already glancing slyly at him to see if he'd rise to the bait; there was no way he could leave before the end of the story without risking everyone laughing at him. Daisy, sensing his dilemma, moved in for the kill.

"Then, suddenly, he heard a noise. It was a giant coal corve – a coal wagon, the biggest one you've ever seen, and it was coming right his way. He stood on the track waiting for it, smiling away, thinking it was kids; you see, he thought that there would be kids pushing it, that they were coming at last, to finally tell him it was home time. He stood up, sore and tired from his day on the door, but so happy at the thought of going up to the sunshine again. And after hearing some terrible, terrible tales of being forgotten, he was as happy as a butcher's dog, that they hadn't forgotten him after all." Daisy gave a theatrical sigh, and some of the little ones sighed too, just to try it out. Some of the older ones wondered what all of this had to do with the butcher's dog (Beamer the butcher's dog was anything but a happy creature, renowned instead for his loud bark and vicious bite), but they managed not to dwell too long on this, though it would carry on puzzling them for weeks.

"He could see the tub rolling towards him, its wheels clanking in the silence of the mine, its little stub of a candle on front, coming closer and closer. Not long now before he'd be up the top, playing with his mates. But ……………….."

The pause seemed to last forever. The children's faces, illuminated by the light from the campfire, looked up expectantly. The smallest girls and boys were now clinging to the bigger girls; preparing themselves for what they knew would be a gruesome finale. Daisy slowly turned around to face them, and slowly took a step towards them. The children leaned forward. "The corve didn't stop; 'cos when it came around the corner there she was, her eyes glittering in the dark; it was the Pit Wife herself pushing the corve from behind, its big iron wheels clanking and groaning as it came towards little Timmy The Tiddler Johnson. He tried to get out of the way, but her eyes fixed him with their horrible stare and, before he knew it, the corve was on top of him." The children gasped in horror, and Tim tried not to feel sick; this wasn't what he wanted to hear.

"That's a stupid story!" His voice came out as a shout as he desperately tried to seem braver than he felt. "That's just a made-up story and I'm not listening to any more," shouted Tim, as he made for the entrance to the cave. He gulped in the fresh clean air and broke into a run, making for the thin line where the beach met the sea. The running made him feel better and, by the time he reached the sea line, the nasty feeling that he'd had in his tummy had abated. Furious with himself for having listened to the story right to its horrible conclusion, he wandered over to a nearby shallow rock pool and angrily began skimming stones.

It wouldn't be that bad, it couldn't be, otherwise they'd never get anyone down the pit. Daisy was the biggest scaredy-cat of all, so she must be making it up or surely she wouldn't work there either? But the damage had been done and now all of the stories he'd been told over the years seemed to be coming back to him this morning. Terrible stories about folks being killed or getting terrible injuries. And then of course there was the sight that everyone in the village dreaded: the sight of the black covered horse-drawn ambulance, making its way from the pit head, usually followed by a line of solemn-looking women and young children. He'd been one of those kids once, straining to see if the victim's head or their feet were hanging out of the back, and remembering the words of the old rhyme:

"Feet mean fit; head means dead."

Chapter 3

Tim fell silent as they reached the entrance to the pit. Dawn had broken now and in the distance, where the deep green of the fields met the horizon, the sky was smeared with streaks of red.

"Right lad," said Jay, bracing himself for what was to come. "That there's Bri the Bank, he'll show you the ropes." Tim's dad pointed to a stocky man wearing a stained white overshirt and a pair of ragged trousers. He didn't look like a boss but seemed to be giving out orders to the assembled men and women who were moving off towards a large hole in the side of the hill.

Daisy turned to Tim. "Try not to cry, our Tim, it's a bit lonely at first but you'll not be by yourself all the time, you'll see the hurriers come past and you can talk to them for a bit." Tim was worried that she was being so nice. That was the second time today she'd been nice to him; she wouldn't be so nice if she knew that he'd already lost her precious gift to him, without even opening it.

"Come on, our kid," said Jo, urging her to hurry up, and, with a quick last glance at Tim, she dismissed him with a quick pat then disappeared over the brow of the hill with the rest of the group.

Bri the Bank lumbered over towards Dad and Tim. He was a large ungainly man whose gruff attitude masked a good heart and a strong sense of responsibility for the boys and girls that worked under him.

"Everybody all right then?"

"Yes sir," replied Tim respectfully.

"Right, well, I'll just run through a few things with you, son, and then we'll go down."

"You got anyone else starting today, Bri?" enquired Tim's dad.

"Yes," said Bri, scratching his head, "as a matter of fact I have. Young Jonnie Wear and his little sister, Evie, it's their first day down as well, and …." The banksman was just about to continue when he was interrupted by a loud scream followed by a familiar chant.

Looking in the direction of the noise, Tim saw a huge group of children assembled around the entrance to the pit.

"Fight, fight, fight!" chanted the group.

Tim had never seen two grown men move so fast as Dad and Bri as they dashed over to the group and pushed their way through to the centre of the circle. Jonnie normally avoided fighting at all costs, but this was different; this was protecting his Evie from two of the biggest bullies in the pit. Although Jonnie wasn't by any means big for his age, he was muscular and quick as a whippet, while Geordie Giles was thick-set and slower. Jonnie danced around Giles, his blond hair swinging loose around his pointed face. Tim had never seen anyone who looked quite like Jonnie, with his elfin face, crystal-blue eyes and slim physique – he looked more like a creature out of one of Mrs Thundertone's picture books: like an elf, or a fairy, rather than a real boy. But there was nothing light or elfin about the way he punched, and, catching the lumbering Geordie a swift left hook, he felled the bigger lad with one blow. The crowd erupted, cheering and egging him on. But before Jonnie could land another blow, strong hands lifted him into the air and plonked him unceremoniously onto the muddy ground.

"What do you think you're playing at, young Wear?" said Bri, with an expression far removed from his normal jovial one.

"It were him, sir," said Jonnie, pointing at the boy sitting on the ground and rubbing his head. "He was saying bad things about my Evie, no one says things about her." His icy blue eyes softened as he picked out her little earnest, anxious face in the crowd.

The banksman loosened his grip on Jonnie and knelt down close to the tiny girl with dark curly hair and huge dark eyes.

"Has he been bullying you, my pet?"

Evie looked solemnly at him, her large brown eyes like saucers, her thumb firmly planted in her rosebud mouth. The thought of this little 'un spending the next twelve hours in the stinking dark pit brought a lump to the banksman's throat.

Slowly the little girl nodded.

"Right, Geordie, it'll be punishment for you lad. Another half shift after today's finishes, and that without pay 'n all." The children gasped: that was one of the worse punishments, to have to work for another six hours, not to finish until ten o'clock at night, then do the long walk back to the village, only to be woken again for work a couple of hours later. Geordie Giles rose from the ground and, pushing his way through the children, paused for a second beside Jonnie. Jonnie flinched at the rotten smell of his hot breath against his cheek.

"I'll get you, Wear, and I'll get your brat 'n all. By the time I've finished, you'll wish the Pit Wife had got you. You'll be sorry you ever crossed me, Wear."

Jonnie flinched, but years of living with Auntie May and Uncle Tom had made him a good actor. He'd learned that bullies loved it when you showed your feelings: it just made them want to hurt you more. Taking Evie's tiny hand in his, he strode purposefully out away from the crowd, his tall elegant figure silhouetted against the brilliant red sky, looking every inch the hero.

Tim was impressed. It took a real man to put Geordie Giles in his place, and not before time too, he thought ruefully, his mind reliving the events of earlier that morning. He'd heard of Jonnie before; how his mam and dad were killed down the mine a long time ago, and how he'd taken care of little Evie ever since. All the same, he was surprised that such a slight, gentle-looking lad could pack a punch like that.

"Right, Jonnie my lad, you and little Evie come over here, with Tim, while I tell you all what you'll be doing today."

Jonnie, Evie and Tim made a motley-looking crew: Jonnie with his long blond hair and elfin looks, Evie with her dark skin and curly hair and Tim, short and stocky, dressed in a pair of saggy woollen trousers and overly big shoes.

Tim hung back for a minute then decided that Jonnie's bravery couldn't go by without him saying something: "Well done mate, back there," he said awkwardly.

The older boy grinned for the first time that day. "Thanks. Geordie Giles has had it coming to him for a long time now, and I doubt that'll be the finish of it. Still," he said, smiling, "not all bad news, is it."

Tim looked in the direction of Jonnie's gaze at the crowd of girls that were giggling, smiling and waving at him.

"Me public, you see, the lasses love a hero," said Jonnie, winking. Waving merrily, Jonnie blew the girls a kiss. "See you later girls," he finished with another roguish wink.

Evie didn't look impressed by the exchange and attached herself to Jonnie's leg, like a limpet to the rocks.

"Scared stiff she is. First day down for both of us."

"How old are you, then?" Tim asked.

"How old do you think I look?" replied Jonnie, puffing out his chest. Tim, anxious not to insult the boy, hesitated. "Oh, at least fourteen?"

"That's right, fourteen, and I'll be fifteen next village day. That is, if I live till then – if Geordie has his way I'll won't make it!"

Tim grinned. "I reckon you and me can sort him out. He's took me birthday present off me."

"You're joking, mate?"

"Naw, he set on me earlier on, stole the present that Daisy bought me."

"That's bad, mate. Is it your birthday then?"

"Yeah, it's today."

"Happy birthday, mate. Tell you what, you and I can hatch a plan to get it back, we'll ...." But before the pair could chat any further, Bri the Bank approached them.

"Right, come on, lads and lasses; it's time to go down now," he said, pointing in the direction of the huge wheel that towered over the pit head. "Let's get in the cage, and I'll tell you what to do when we get to the bottom."

Evie started to cry, clinging pitifully to Jonnie's loose trousers.

"Give over, man," said Jonnie, gently. "We'll be ok, won't we Tim?"

Tim put on a brave face that he hoped wouldn't betray the terrible sick feeling that he still had in the pit of his stomach. "Aye, it'll be a laugh down there, the three of us, a real old laugh, specially if Jonnie there brings all them lasses down!" Jonnie grinned. "Oh, them lasses, I can't get away from them!"

"Right," said Bri, "take your tallies." He handed them each a metal disc with numbers on it. Jonnie's expression darkened as he took the cold metal coin and hung it around his neck. None of them needed to be told what these were for: if there was an accident in the pit, this may be the only thing that would be left of them. Jonnie gulped back a sob as he remembered collecting his mam's tally from the pit head; this was the job he'd swore he and Evie would never have to do, yet here they were, only four years later, about to descend into the gloomy hole.

The cage groaned as Bri pulled open the metal doors and they stepped into the gloom. The trio fell quiet as the lift went down, the silence broken only by the creaking and groaning of the lift as it descended into the blackness. Before long the clean air was replaced by a terrible acrid smell, the smell of rotten eggs. It got right to the back of your throat, giving you a horrible choking feeling.

"What's that?" croaked Tim. "It stinks down here, worse than the netty[3] in the yard."

"That'll only be a bit of firedamp," said Bri with a grin. "Bad gases that sneak along these passages looking for places to hide: that's why you've got the most important job in the mine, opening the traps so they can escape." Bri stopped and turned to the crew: "Right, You'll be working door three, our Tim, and Jonnie you'll be on door five. I'll put Evie on door four so you'll not be too far off each other."

---

[3] Geordie word for a toilet

"Where will you be, Dad?" demanded Tim, turning to Jay.

"Not too far, son; you just concentrate on your own stuff and the day will go by quick enough," said Jay, ruffling Tim's hair affectionately. Tim was fiercely proud of his dad's reputation as the best getter in the mine; he could hack more coal from the face than anyone else in there. Tim had heard the men in the pub after work shaking their heads at Jay's prowess. But the work came at a high price: each day when Jay came in from the pit, it was Tim's job to fill the old tin bath for him, then take the scrubbing brush and scrub Jay's back until it was red raw. Even after half an hour of this, his dad's back would still be blue with the coal dust that had been rubbed into the terrible wounds caused by rubbing up against the cruel rocks.

The jolt as the cage hit the bottom of the mine knocked them all off balance and Tim landed hard against Jonnie.

"Howay man, there's no hope for you if you can't stand up before yer shift." Tim smiled in spite of his fear. Jonnie was a one all right: he seemed to be able to laugh at anything.

"Right, lads and lasses," said Bri firmly, "I'll just light me midgy, and we'll be away."

Bri picked up a box-like object with what looked like a little candle in the middle and, lighting the candle, he illuminated the dark passage ahead and led the party forward.

It was black all right, blacker than anything Tim had ever experienced. Apart from Bri's midgy lamp there was not even a flicker of light.

Already Tim found he had to bend over; Bri and Dad were virtually on their hands and knees as they moved down the passageway. A couple of times Tim caught his head on the overhanging rocks above.

"How much further, sir?" enquired Jonnie.

"Not too far now, lad, we'll be going downhill for a bit in a while; then it won't be far till we get to your door."

Tim's back was starting to ache, and he felt something warm and wet dribble down his cheeks. He supposed it must be blood, but there was no light to see the colour. His feet, not used to the heavy clogs, were beginning to blister, and he suddenly realised that they were soaked through. Bending down to feel the ground his hand met water. Water, he was up to his knees in water!

Horror gripped his stomach like a vice: not water, surely he wouldn't have to sit in water for twelve hours.

He felt tears of self-pity start to roll down his cheeks, and the most miserable feeling washed over him in waves.

"Don't leave me, Jonnie." Evie's quiet voice interrupted his own misery. "Don't leave me here in the wet, Jonnie."

Tim couldn't see Jonnie's face, but he knew, if it had been his own Lottie or Mary, he couldn't have brought them down into this dark, stinking blackness. Bri came to a sudden halt at a door set low in the rock. By the light of his lamp, they could just make out a rope dangling from the roof.

Just beside the door, there was a small indentation in the rock. Bri turned to Evie: "This is where you'll be sitting, my lamb." He pointed at the indentation. "Now, Wear, you just explain to your lass there what she has to do." Jonnie bent down to his sister; by the flickering light of the midgy lamp his face looked more ethereal than ever, his sculpted cheekbones casting elfin shadows on the black walls. Tim couldn't see the expression in his eyes, but he could hear the tremor in his voice.

"This is where you sit, Evie. When you hear a noise then that'll be the corve full of coal coming and you need to pull on this rope to open the door."

Evie's eyes were wide with terror. "Please, Jonnie, please stay, stay with us; I promise I'll be good."

Jonnie knelt down to her with a tenderness that made Tim wince, and held her little hand in his. "You've got to remember to close the door, our Evie, close the door when the corve has passed through it, so that the bad gases can pass through and it will be safe."

Tim glanced at Bri the Bank, who was starting to get impatient, his bad feelings about leaving this little girl down here making him gruff.

"Do you understand?" His booming voice sounded even louder in the narrow passage, and Evie shrank back in terror.

"Leave her, sir." Jonnie took a step forward and, in one swift movement, removed Evie's hand from his sleeve. "I'll come for you when the last corve is done, I promise."

The children could still hear Evie's crying as they moved off down the passage. It was too low for them to stand now and even Tim had to get down on his hands and knees and crawl through the filthy water. The stench was unbearable now and he was glad he'd sicked up the remains of his breakfast earlier. Evie's cries weren't the only noises in the pit. There were great clanking and booming noises and occasional loud shouts and cries. They seemed to come from a long way away, echoing in the long passageways.

Suddenly the banksman lifted his midgy lamp up to his face and turned to Jay. "This is it then, mate."

Jay turned to Tim and shone his own light in Tim's face. "Take care, lad, and do a good job. I'll see you again at home time."

"How will I know when it's time to go home, Dad?"

"Don't you worry: the hurriers will come and tell you when to pack up," said Jay patiently, turning away from the group. He gave Tim a quick pat on the shoulder then disappeared into the blackness.

The Bri turned to Jonnie and Tim. "You make sure them doors is closed, mind you, no sleeping on the job." And he added sternly: "You forget to close those doors and you'll see the whole mine blown to blazes; remember the bad gases, and if you smell bad eggs, you need to waft the draft." His face was hard now as he turned from being the friendly man at the pit head to the mine taskmaster, his dark eyes cold and fathomless.

"What's waft the draft, sir?" replied Tim.

"That's opening and shutting your door, so that the gases get wafted through," explained Bri.

"We won't let you down, sir," said Tim. "Us Carters know what we have to do."

"And you?" said Bri, looking at Jonnie.

Jonnie looked Bri straight in the eye. "You can count on me and Evie."

"Aye, well, mebbies I can and mebbies I can't, we'll see. Any road, you can stop here. Your mate Tim here will be down the passage at the low mine apart from your little sister there; he's the only one what will fit the roof's that low."

As Bri turned away, Jonnie caught the look on Tim's face.

"Howay mate, it'll be all right, and before we know it we'll be back up top there with the lasses, and planning a beating for Geordie again!"

Tim grinned weakly. Trust Jonnie to put a brave face on it. Bri grimaced as he heard the two lads whispering. He was used to taking children down the pit, and he liked to think of them like his own, to look out for them and be like a dad to them while they were away from their own parents. But, for some reason, he felt bad about this crew. It was what his wife would call one of them funny feelings that something wasn't quite right. He'd been feeling funny for a while: it started with the magpie that landed on his prize leeks just yesterday. One for sorrow – he always remembered his nan saying that. He'd chased it away, but the uneasy feeling was still with him.

Most kids settled after a while, and some took to it like ducks to water. Annie Giles: he remembered the day she'd started work. No crying for her, though she'd only been three years old when her mam brought her down. A funny little thing, short hair like a lad, and a serious little face on her, like a little old lady in a kid's body. Normally the mams were upset when it came to leaving their little ones by the traps. Not Martha though: her hard face was blank as she handed Annie to the banksman. "Remember, you do as he tells you," said Martha, handing over a small bait tin. "Clip her if she gives you trouble." With that, she made off down the narrow passage; not a wave or a kiss or even a pat on the head was proffered to the tiny girl with the serious face. When he left her at the trap door where she'd be working, she listened to his instructions silently, before taking her place beside the door. She was a strange one all right.

Later that day, when the time came for the shift to knock off, he'd normally just leave it to the hurriers to tell the trappy lads and lasses that it was going-home time, but this time he had wanted to make sure that the little 'un was all right. When he arrived at the door where he had left her twelve hours before, she was sitting exactly as he'd left her, still holding tightly to the stub of candle she'd saved from the morning. Leading her out of the mine in silence, he deposited her at the pit head to wait for her mother. In the sunlight, she looked even more like a little old lady, with her thin hair and a pale face, wan and thin. It was then that he noticed the large black bruises covering her arms and legs. He sighed at the memory. She was a hard 'un, that Martha. Oh, she hadn't had it easy, there was no doubt about that, but still, no reason to knock the lass about.

Tim watched as the faint light from the candle disappeared into the distance. Holding his meagre bait to his chest, he wondered how on earth he was going to keep it dry until it was time to eat it. How long would he be able to last out hunched over like this? How long would it be before his legs gave out and he collapsed back into the water? He couldn't believe that he was going to have to sit in all that water – it stank too. No netty down here … he guessed he'd just have to go where he stood. Clutching his candle stub to him he longed to be back up top again, smelling clean fresh air instead of the disgusting rank smell that assailed his nostrils now.

He wondered what Mam was doing. It was Monday, so it would be wash day: she'd take the washing and give it a good scrub in the tub out in the yard. Tim liked wash day, there was always a nice smell in the little house when he got home: a fresh soapy smell. Thinking of the lovely soapy smell made Tim even more aware of the disgusting smells around him. It was getting hard to breathe, the air was so muggy and damp, and something, it must be the dark water, was stinking really badly; he didn't even want to imagine what it might be. Lost in thought, Tim hardly noticed when Bri's midgy lamp stopped short in front of him.

"Here we are lad, it's your door."

Pausing in front of a low wooden trap door, Bri pulled a slimy rope from the dirty water. "This is what you need to pull when the corves come through."

"That's all ye need to do, dead easy for a big lad like you." Tim couldn't see if Bri was smiling, but his voice sounded jolly through the darkness. How could he sound so happy when he was leaving them all to this for twelve hours a day? Tim felt as if he was going to cry. The water was up to his knees now and his back was sore where he'd bumped it on the low ceilings. His bait tin was slung around his waist on a belt, so at least that would be safe from the rising waters.

He managed to summon up the words to thank the banksman, who was standing there expectantly.

"Thanks sir, see you later," he muttered.

Bri gave Tim a quick pat on the shoulder and turned around. Tim watched his light as it disappeared into the darkness, then turned and felt for the space where he would sit for the next twelve hours. The blackness down the mine was complete. There wasn't even a chink of light. He felt for the rope. It was slimy and warm like a horrible big worm in his hand. He'd better not let it slip or he'd never find it again in this darkness. His back was killing him and he was already tempted to sit down in the water. But if he did that, then what would happen to his bait? It would get wet, and then he'd have nothing to eat until he got home. He was starving now and wondered how long it had taken them to get this far down the mine. He thought of his bait tin and the nice piece of bread and jam he'd seen his mam packing this morning. His jacket bulged with his water bottles. Dad often took a jar of jam down with him; he coughed nearly all the time now and often brought up black dust with it. He said that the jam helped him breathe better and that Mam's plum jam made it better. Suddenly Tim heard a rumbling noise deep in the tunnels. Terrified, he flattened himself against the wall. Was this the Pit Wife coming to get him already?

The noise grew louder: it seemed to be coming closer to him. The rumbling turned into a roar and the ground underneath his feet seemed to shake.

Feeling the cold rocks on either side of the passageway, he started to move away from the door, his feet slipping in the slimy mud. He groped for his pit rat but his hands shook so badly he couldn't light it. Feeling for the rope, he managed to regain his balance. He wasn't going to sit around and let the Pit Wife get him. He was off.

* * *

Just as Tim was about to drop his rope and run for it, he heard someone shout: "Hoy, new lad, open up then slow coach!"

It seemed to be coming from the other side of the trap door. His heart pounding, he realised that it was a boy's voice, so it couldn't be the Pit Wife, could it?

The thick slimy rope in his hand brought him back to reality. The voice was more insistent now.

"Come on then, our Tim, take all day won't you."

Giving the rope a good tug, he swung the heavy wooden door open and there, illuminated by the light of a single candle, was the smiling face of his brother Jo.

"What are ye doing, bonny lad," said Jo, grinning. "Thought it was the Pit Wife come to get yer?" he laughed.

Tim felt silly now and tried to sound as if he'd never been afraid in the first place. "Oh yeah, but now I see it was a scarier looking version," he managed to retort. "Where's our Daisy then?" he demanded.

"She'll be along in a bit. Bad news though, mate. She's working with the Giles girl."

Tim's face fell as he thought about Annie; she couldn't have ended up with anyone worse.

Just then another filthy blackened face popped up from behind the corve.

"Hello slowcoach, got the easy job then," grinned Jane.

Tim blushed. Jane had been working as a hurrier for five years now but Tim knew her as one of the kids that hung around with Daisy. She was a right tease, was Jane, always teasing him – but in a nice way.

She took a filthy rag from out of her pocket and wiped away the sweat on her face.

"Working for yer dad today, Tim. Worst job in the pit, he's a right slave driver 'n all," she grinned. "Come on then, Slowcoach Jo, time to get back to work."

Jane disappeared behind the corve and Jo lowered himself into the filthy water until he was on his hands and knees. Tim winced when he saw the way that the heavy chain cut into Jo's legs, and the look on his face told Tim he had one of his headaches again.

"Wait, our Jo," shouted Tim. "Give us a light before you go?"

Jo heaved himself up into a crouching position and, holding out his candle, lowered the flame onto the cold wick. "There ye are, you've got that pit rat for a while there lad, don't waste it!"

Then, putting his head to the ground, his chains taut, he disappeared out of sight.

Tim crouched, his candle in his hand, the hot wax running down his frozen fingers. He was alone again now. The rumbling sound of the corve echoed into the distance.

He looked at the candle, remembering that his mam had told him not to waste it, and with a single breath he blew it out.

* * *

Daisy's head was down, her hands and feet immersed in muddy water. Behind her, the heavy corve slowly inched forward along the narrow rails.

Another girl pushed at the corve from behind, her blonde head pressed hard against the back of the wooden tub, her feet struggling to maintain purchase on the sloppy mud. It was only the fifth corve this morning and they would be expected to heave at least another fifteen before the end of their shift. The corve clanked and groaned as the heavy iron wheels inched up the steep slope. Her stomach rumbled and reminded her that she hadn't eaten since breakfast time. When she was a trappy lass she'd been able to eat whenever she felt hungry, but in this new job she would have to wait until the lunch break to get out her bait. She had heard that some getters didn't allow their hurriers to take more than ten minutes before they were chained back up to the corves and set about their work again.

* * *

"Come on, useless."

Annie's shrill voice goaded her on. Annie was strong and pushed the corves hard. This meant that Daisy had to keep pace or risk being knocked into by the heavy tub. Her knees were hurting her now: she couldn't see the stones and loose pieces of gravel that lay beneath the filthy water and her bare knees were at the mercy of the sharp gravel. She understood now: understood what Jo had been talking about all that time; understood that he wasn't a coward, that animals in the field were treated better than them. Too late, she realised that this was her future; bound and chained like an animal, living in the darkness until she died. Even after she got married and had children she'd be back down here in a short while, her children and her children's children suffering the same fate.

Pulling on the chain, she wondered how Tim was getting on. She remembered her first day at the mine. She remembered the darkness, sitting in her little corner beside the door, wondering when her first corve would come through. She remembered eating her bait really quickly and then being starving for the rest of the day. But it wasn't like this. It wasn't painful and hard like this job. She'd never felt as if she couldn't go on, like with this work. She really didn't know how she could go on: the chain was cutting into her thighs, she was soaked through and the leather belt cut into her tummy like a knife.

"You're the worst lass I've ever worked with, Carter. You're a lazy good-fer-nothing just like yer stupid brother, crying and whingeing like him 'n all. Me and Geordie Giles are going to do for him when we get out later. Stupid wimp with his stupid parcel."

Daisy was used to name-calling, and she knew that when she was partnered with Annie there would be trouble, but when Annie mentioned a parcel her ears pricked up.

"What parcel you talking about?"

"Ha, that got you going didn't it! The parcel we took from little boy Carter this morning."

The two girls were working at opposite ends of the coal truck so Daisy couldn't see if Annie was telling the truth or not, but Annie couldn't have known about her present to Tim unless she'd met him that morning, and somehow managed to steal it.

"You're lying, Giles. You always lie."

"Am I lying, am I?" sung Annie in that sing-songy voice Daisy hated. "Come on then, hard lass – you come up my end and see if I'm lying."

Daisy knew that once she took off her chains and faced Annie, that would be it; there would be no avoiding a fight, and Annie was strong, really strong.

"Shut your gob, Giles," shouted Daisy.

"Oh big talker now, eh? Least I haven't got a brother who's soft in the head," retorted Annie, her voice cutting through the rumble of the corve as it moved along the track. "And another one who everybody laughs at – old baldy Joey Carter," she chanted in a sing-song voice.

Suddenly Daisy snapped. She wasn't normally given to hitting people, but standing there, her back aching from the unaccustomed work, chained and tethered like an animal, the leather and steel cutting into her legs mixing blood with filthy black water and coal dust, she felt a red-hot anger, so red-hot that for a moment she forgot her fear. Stopping short, she unclipped her belt and made her way to the back of the cart where Annie was crouching in the filthy water, her filthy face glowing with coal dust by the dim candlelight in the cart.

"Show it to me," said Daisy, her normally pleasant face screwed up in anger.

Annie smirked. Daisy didn't scare her: she was used to a daily beating from her drunken mother, and nothing could be worse than that. "Come here, you little wimp."

Daisy moved forward; she couldn't bear the thought that her precious present to Tim may have fallen into the hands of this horrible girl. It wasn't much, but she'd saved up for months to buy it.

Annie grinned, holding out her hand, and there on her filthy palm was a tiny silver wren, the chain catching in the candle light.

"Give it here," growled Daisy menacingly as she moved towards the crouching girl.

"In your dreams, pet," grinned Annie, closing her fist. "It's mine now; you'll have to fight me for it."

As Daisy took another step towards her, Annie unclipped her chain and with one swift movement drew it back and swung it with all her might at Daisy, catching her across the eye and splitting open her cheek.

Daisy reeled back in agony, stunned from the blow. As she fell to the ground, Annie prepared to strike again.

* * *

Tim had given up trying to crouch down and now sat in water up to his waist. His bread and jam were long gone and he'd already started on his second bottle of water. He was getting used to the corves coming through and looked forward to the deep rumbling that signalled the next one and a friendly face peering through the darkness at him. He'd never spent so much time alone before and found it strange. He'd started to make up little songs to tunes that he knew, adapting the words to people that he knew and some of the funny stuff that went with them. His mind wandered and he imagined himself on the surface, running across the fields with his mates, warm and dry, enjoying the feeling of the sun on his bare chest and arms. He thought about his birthday dinner and wondered if he would be having any meat with it. Last year his mam had cut up a scrunchy apple and they'd each had a piece, loving the sweet juiciness of it. He wondered about Evie and Jonnie, what they were doing each sitting in their space beside their trap doors, wondered if Evie was still crying.

The rumbling sound of a corve disturbed his daydreams and he got ready with the rope. The door swung open and he saw the faint light of a candle coming towards him. The hurrier really looked to be in trouble – he or she, he couldn't quite make out, was pressed flat to the floor and the corve looked to be about to crash into them. As they came through the narrow doorway the hurrier raised her head.

Daisy was barely recognisable, her filthy face was covered in blood and hot tears poured down her cheeks.

"She's got your present, Tim, she's got it, your special thing," sobbed Daisy.

"Aw, tell her to dry up, the soppy moo," snarled Annie from the back of the corve.

"What have you done to her, you miserable witch!" shouted Tim.

Annie Giles appeared from behind the corve, wiping her face with a rag. Her mean eyes shone in the candlelight which illuminated her sharp foxy features.

"Get pulling, Carter, or I'll tell me mam of her, then she'll be for it."

"Give it back," shouted Tim, pushing his face into Annie's.

"Don't, Tim," cried Daisy, "she'll chain you, like she did me."

Just as Annie began to draw back her chain again, Daisy leapt from the front of the cart, and landed squarely on top of the wretched girl. Annie, taken by surprise and momentarily winded, dropped the silver object into the dark water. It had all but disappeared, but Tim, emboldened by Daisy's actions, darted forward and retrieved the precious object.

"Take it, Daisy, take it and get out of here," he shouted. "She'll kill you when she gets up."

"But what about the corve, Tim, who'll pull the corve?"

Tim put his arm awkwardly around his sister's thin shoulders as she sobbed.

"Let me worry about that," hissed Tim. "Now just go, go to the cave and wait for me there. Don't let Mam see the state of your face."

Daisy needed no second bidding and hugged her brother tightly, before disappearing down the dark passage.

"Well, chicken boy," said Annie as she clambered to her knees. "Who's gonna pull me corve now eh? Cos the next door's the one me mam works on, and you know what'll happen if we don't show up to take her coal. Put the belt on," she said menacingly. "Put the belt on and pull the corve or me mam will kill you and me both."

Tim hesitated for a second: he knew that to leave the door would be very dangerous. The poisonous gases may build up and cause a terrible explosion – but if he didn't do as Annie said, then Daisy and he would be in for the beating of their lives.

"Did ye not hear me, stupid, I say put the belt on and get going." Annie was more insistent now; her voice was shrill as it echoed around the stone passageway.

Tim reluctantly took hold of the leather belt and fastened it slowly around his waist. The chain came between his legs and as he lowered himself to the ground he felt the weight of the corve pulling at his slim frame. Casting a last look at the door that he'd promised to guard, he began to pull. Every muscle felt like it was tearing apart as he heaved at the corve, but try as he might he couldn't shift it. Without pads on, there was nothing to protect his knees from the loose shale that lined the floor of the mine and he winced in pain as the stones cut through his trousers. After what seemed like an age the corve finally began to inch its way along the passageway, its iron wheels clanking in the stillness of the mine.

Behind them, the door swung shut, but without anyone to hold it in place the rickety hinges groaning under the weight of the wet wood grew tired of holding up the dead weight, and with a creak and a sigh they allowed the door to open again. It only opened a little; just a chink, but the evil-smelling gases only needed a tiny space to silently pour through into the next passage. Making their way to the roof they passed as far along the passage as they could before becoming trapped; and there they stopped: blocked at gate four.

Chapter 4

Daisy stumbled down the passageway, feeling her way through the blackness. The relief that she had felt at being released from the chain and belt was now replaced by dull fear. What would her dad say when he found out? And what would Ma Giles say when she found out that one of her hurriers had done a bunk? Daisy knew she'd be in for a beating from both of them, but this was nothing compared to the thought of her mam's face when she found out. She could just picture it now; crumpled and upset with crying. And what about Dad? He'd be so ashamed. He'd be like he was with Jo, so downcast that she'd let him down: he would be the laughing stock of the mine. And what would happen about their house? Since Mam had had to give up working at the mine, they relied on the money that Daisy, Jo and now Tim would be bringing in. Dad earned a good wage but, with four little ones at home and another on the way, it wasn't enough to keep them all in food and rent.

Pausing for a moment, she heard a dull rumble of a corve coming towards her; panicking, she frantically felt for a gap in the rock that might provide a hiding place. The last thing she wanted was for other hurriers to know that she'd run away; the story would be round the mine in no time and then they'd all be after her. The corve was approaching fast now: she could see the dim light of its front candle. Turning away from the sound, she frantically felt her way along the narrow passageway, desperately trying to keep her footing in the slimy water. As she rounded a corner in the darkness, a dim light shone out from the rock. Gasping in fear she hung back, thinking it was someone lurking in the darkness, but as her eyes got used to the dim lighting she saw that it was only Connie the canary's cage. Remembering back to earlier that day, she suddenly realised that the cage was hanging in a small indentation in the rock, just big enough for a girl to squeeze behind. Feeling her way along the slimy rock, she edged towards it.

* * *

Evie had stopped her sobbing when she finally realised that Jonnie wasn't coming back to get her. She'd eaten the cheese sandwiches that he had made before leaving that morning and now she was starving. She'd noticed little squeaking noises all around her and wondered what they were. Then she felt the patter of tiny claws on her arm. She wasn't afraid of rats; they had plenty of them back at home. Her uncle kept chickens in their back yard and the rats were always sniffing around the chickens' corn. There were sometimes rats inside too: her Auntie May didn't keep a very clean house, unlike some of the other women in the street. The floor was often covered in crumbs and dirt that she left there from one week to the next. Evie often wished that she lived in a nice house like Mrs Appleridge next door, and spent long hours dreaming of what her mum's house would have been like had she not died when Evie was a baby. She shivered; she was sitting in cold water up to her waist and however she sat or knelt she just couldn't get comfortable. For a while she'd even tried standing up but it was so tiring not being able to stand fully straight that she gave up after a while and sank back down into the filthy water. She longed to be back in the sunshine again and wondered if it was nearly time to go home. Thinking about the sunshine reminded her that she was missing Jonnie and she choked back a little sob. As far back as she could remember, Jonnie had always been there for her. She couldn't really remember her mam and dad – she'd only been tiny when they'd died – and they'd had to travel hundreds of miles from their village to come and live with Auntie May and Uncle Tom.

If they'd known what it would be like they'd have done anything to avoid coming. They didn't have a bedroom but slept in a little cupboard under the stairs. It was always cold and smelly in the cottage, and there was never enough to eat. In spite of the fact that there always seemed to be more than enough food for their auntie and uncle, Jonnie and she were forced to live on gruel and leftovers from their aunt and uncle's table. Her stomach growled and she stifled a yawn: she was sleepy, so sleepy, the cold water seeped through her thick gaiters and was numbing her legs. Surely it couldn't harm just to have a little sleep ....

Chapter 5

Jonnie sat in the pitch black. He was so bored that he'd taken to reciting little songs he'd learned at the Sunday school and was trying to put his own words into them. He'd known that it would be boring down here, but he hadn't thought that it would be this bad. He wasn't used to being alone; he and Evie had been inseparable since their mum and dad died in that pit accident when he was ten. He'd never forget that day. He'd been playing in the street outside their house. Mam and Dad both worked down the pit; Mam was a hurrier and Dad a getter. Jonnie had often offered to go down the pit to work but his mam and dad had rather that he stay home a bit longer and look after Evie. The first he'd known of the accident was when they saw the horse-drawn ambulance making its way down the cobbled streets towards the mine. He'd been playing with much younger kids, making them laugh with jokes and funny faces.

"Look everybody, it's the ambulance, someone must have copped it down the mine," shouted Suzie Wambrick, pointing at the horse-drawn ambulance that looked to be heading towards the pit head.

The children formed a disorderly line behind the vehicle and solemnly followed it to the entrance. By the time they arrived, a small crowd had gathered at the top of the shaft. The children fought their way to the front of the group where a man was holding court.

"Now don't panic, there's been a bit of an accident, that's all. Nothing to worry about," he added, trying to look reassuring, but the crowd weren't convinced.

"Just stop messing with us and tell us what's happened," shouted a lady, her shawl pulled tightly around her shoulders, a baby's head just peeping out from underneath it.

"Aye, we can see there's been an accident, we're not stupid, man, just tell us what happened," added an old woman, her face furrowed with concern.

The ambulance driver pushed his way to the front of the group.

"Where are they then?"

"We haven't got them out yet mate, so you aren't needed yet," growled the banksman.

"Someone needs to be doing something to get them out, instead of just standing here," shouted the old woman.

"What's happened?" cried the children anxiously.

"We think there are about twenty of them trapped down there but there could be more. The deputy's doing a head count now, so we should find out soon, who's alive and who's not," whispered the old lady to her friend.

"Right, who's coming down with me?" shouted the banksman. "I need as many able bodies as I can get, it's going to take some work to get them out of there."

For a minute there was silence then a chorus of voices all shouted at once, "I'll go," "Yes I'm ready to go down."

"Count me in." The tall slim girl with the elfin face and long blonde hair stepped forward. "I'll go, sir, I want to go: Mum and Dad are down there."

The banksman completely ignored the plea: it was as if the child had never spoken.

"All able-bodied men and lads, all of you, I need all of you down there."

The child shrank back, blushing with fury and shame.

"You stay with us up top," said the lady kindly. "Better that way, there'll be plenty for us to do when they bring them up top."

The girl turned away, her blue eyes cold now with fury. Just because she was a girl, she wasn't allowed to go and help her mam and dad; no one would have stopped a lad. So she had to sit there for three long days with the women and small children while the men and boys arrived from villages far and wide to help with the search.

And it was three long days before they finally brought them up; three days of sitting day and night at the bank head as body after body was raised to the surface. Three days sitting there uselessly with the women and children, while down below the rescuers fought their way through rock and stone to free the gas. Gas, they said it was, a pocket of trapped gas that caused an explosion. One of the little 'uns had fallen asleep and forgotten to open the trap. Part of the pit roof had fallen in at the section where his mum and dad had been working. They never stood a chance.

It was just before the funeral that the girl cut off her hair. A rainy November day and already almost dark at three o'clock. Her sister was with a neighbour, and she sat alone in the house. It was silent, so silent: apart from the steady ticking of her mum's wooden clock, there was nothing. The grate where a cosy warm fire once warmed her, as she sat beside her mum in the evening, listening to stories about when her mother was little, was now cold and dark, the grey ash spilling onto the bright clippie mat. She shivered and, drawing her shawl around her thin shoulders, made her way towards the back door. She hadn't been in her mum's little shed out the back since she died. Part of her thought that, the longer she stayed out of it, the longer she could imagine that her mum was out there, reading her tarot cards for one of the village women; that she'd be indoors soon, busying about making the tea. But today suddenly she needed to be in there, with her mum's precious objects: her beautiful shawls, and the bright painted china that had come with her when she moved out of her family's caravan and into a proper house for the first time in her life. At first the villagers hadn't liked it: they didn't trust Gypsies. But Josephine was so gentle and kind that one by one the women started to warm to her. When they found out about her special gifts, they couldn't keep away from her house. That was when Dad had built her the little shed, out in the back yard just beside the netty.

"You can't have all and sundry coming tramping in here at all hours, gel," he announced one evening, after a steady stream of women with all sorts of questions and problems had arrived on their doorstep.

"They don't want us lot hearing their private business. And besides," he added, "if you're going to tell their fortunes you have to do it properly and get them to pay you fair and square. Cross your palm with a bit of the old silver, as your nan used to say," he grinned.

He had started to build the shed the very next day. At first Josephine thought it was a bad idea.

"It'll be so small, and so cold in the winter," she whispered in her daughter's ear.

But her husband carried on regardless, and little by little the shed took shape.

The girl lit the candle and crossed the dark yard, slowly turning the key in the lock.

As the door swung open, the candle threw strange shadows onto the dark walls. Apart from a damp smell, it was all exactly as her mother had left it. Closing the door, she lowered herself into her mum's chair, her tired body sinking into the rich red cushions. Her fingers lightly traced the brightly coloured embroidered peacocks that adorned the Gypsy shawls which hung loosely over the chair. The crystal was still there in the middle of the table, its dark depths illuminated by the weak candlelight.

As she stared at it, it seemed to get brighter and, the longer she looked, the brighter it became. She rubbed her eyes: she'd hardly slept a wink since they died. Maybe her eyes were playing up. But no, there it was again, glowing in the dark, except now the glow seemed to be coming from deep within the ball, and yes, as she peered more closely, it wasn't just yellow but a swirling rainbow orb, pulsating in the darkness. Suddenly she heard a soft voice. "Come closer," whispered the voice. It seemed to be coming from the crystal, beckoning her on.

"We'll show you the way. Come closer, Joanna, come closer." There seemed to be more than one voice now: a chorus of children's voices, calling her name.

As she gazed into the globe, a tiny figure appeared to her. At first she thought it was just her reflection – it looked like her, but there was something different about this girl: this girl had shorter hair hanging just below the ears. She was scruffy and tired-looking, with a cut just below her left eye. Peering closer she gasped; it wasn't a girl. It was a boy; a boy that looked just like her! Mesmerised now, she realised that he was holding something: glinting and glittering in the glassy globe was a silver wren.

The voices were louder now, rising to a chorus. "Fly, Jonnie, fly," they shouted. "Escape from the dark, or die in the dark," they commanded.

As she gazed, the lights began to fade and before she knew it the globe once again had grown dark and still.

As if in a trance, she moved towards her mother's sewing table and carefully opened the drawer. Taking out her mother's precious scissors, with slow careful movements, she sliced off her hair, cutting through the blonde tresses with clean, quick strokes. Then, carefully replacing the scissors, she picked up the candle, locked the door and crossed the yard to the house. By the time she reached the kitchen she had decided: the girl that she had been was dead forever; from now on she would be Jonnie, a boy afraid of nothing. Jonnie the boy would take care of her little sister Evie and make sure that neither of them ever ended up dying in the dark like their parents. They may be dead and gone now but he could at least make sure that Evie was safe.

Chapter 6

It had been easy after that. It was only a short time after the funeral that they went to live with their Aunt May and Uncle Tom. She knew that Dad had a brother and that he was married and lived far away from them. She had heard Dad and Mum whispering together about people from the North. She gathered from her father's tone that her aunt and uncle didn't have any time for her mum's people, and that they hadn't heard from them since Jonnie was born. It was the money that made them decide to look after Jonnie and Evie. Mum and Dad had a small amount saved up and, what with the sale of the furniture from the house, she knew there'd be a tidy amount for anyone who took them on.

It took them two days to get to Skry, and by the time they arrived you would never have known that Jonnie was really a girl. Her face was filthy from the travel and she had adopted an old pair of her dad's trousers, cut down and belted to fit. Although a couple of men from the village had come most of the way with them, they travelled the last leg of the journey with an old carrier, so there was no one to give away her secret. Evie was none the wiser: too young to realise that her sister had decided to become her brother, she grew up believing that nothing had ever been any different.

* * *

From the very first day they arrived Jonnie hated Auntie May; she was a thin-featured woman who had a nasty tongue on her. She had started off working in a weaving factory but had to give up, owing to a mysterious illness that struck her suddenly and meant that she couldn't work. The local women said it was less of an illness and more like the 'lazy bug'. From then on, all she did was sit in the chair all day and drink out of a green bottle that she hid from Uncle Tom. Unlike the other sparkling clean cottages in the row, theirs was filthy and stank of rank food and old turnips. It wasn't helped by the smell of Charlie, the pig that they kept in the yard, and who often wandered in, looking for food to add to the starvation rations imposed by May and Tom. Auntie May didn't seem to notice; whatever it was in the green bottle, by lunchtime she'd be snoring her head off while Charlie snuffled around the kitchen picking up any scraps that he could find.

Uncle Tom laboured at a nearby farm and left the house at four o'clock each morning. He was rarely home before sunset, and when he did get home Jonnie and Evie knew to keep out of his way. His temper had never been good at the best of times, but after the children moved in it was worse than ever. Tom wasn't a bad man but years of living with Miserable May (as the villagers nicknamed her) had ground him down and made him into the foul-tempered man that the children had come to know and hate.

Jonnie had had to grow up quickly and keep Evie safe from their auntie and uncle. She loved the little sister that she'd raised from being a baby, and most people were used to seeing her in Jonnie's arms. She couldn't bear it when Evie cried and would do anything to make her laugh; that's how she became known as a bit of a joke. Always having a laugh, always taking the mickey – no wonder Jonnie was so popular with the other children. She didn't feel like joking now though: now all she could think about was that they would both be trapped underground like Mum and Dad, never seeing the sunshine, never able to go to the seaside or have any adventures, just stuck here in the dark until they got old and grey. She'd always dreamed about getting away from Skry village, getting away and travelling to a place called London, a place where you could have adventures and find work. She dreamed about taking Evie away, and starting a new life away from their auntie and uncle. She would have to do something soon: she was growing up now and she wouldn't be able to hide the fact she wasn't the boy everyone thought she was for much longer. Even little Evie was bound to guess sooner or later.

* * *

"Open up!" The shout brought her back to the present and she quickly pulled on the rope. The door creaked slowly open and the figure pulling the corve started to pass through. The light from the candle on the front of the corve briefly lit up the hurrier's face.

"Tim?" The face was almost unrecognisable as that of the boy that she'd left just a few hours earlier. Tim's face was streaked with dirt and sweat, his eyes were wild with fear, and his hair was plastered to his scalp.

"What's happened?" she whispered in horror. "What are you doing pulling that corve?"

Tim raised his head and Jonnie spotted the terror in his eyes.

"It's me sister Daisy, she's done a bunk and there's nobody to pull her corve so I've had to do it."

"But what about your door? What about the gases?" she gasped.

"Nothing'll happen to the door." Annie appeared from behind the corve. "He'll do what I tell him and pull this in place of his stupid sister."

"But the gases! There'll be nothing to stop the gases and we'll all be blown to pieces," said Jonnie, aghast at what Tim had done.

"Aw shut up you, what do you know about this place? I've been working here all my life and you come in and think you know it all. Hurriers'll shut the door after they've hurried through it. Now get on with it," said Annie, with a toss of her head, as she disappeared back behind the corve and began to push.

"Open the door, Wear," commanded Annie.

"I'll open the door all right," replied Jonnie grimly. "But it'll probably be for the last time mind, and when I'm done, Annie, you'll be sorry you ever started all of this."

"What are you doing?" demanded Tim.

"The only thing I can do: go and get Evie before this place blows sky high."

A snort came from behind the corve. "Typical of you lot, off at the first sign of trouble," said Annie. "There won't be no explosion. Doors have been left before when kids fall asleep, and nothing happens. It's just weaklings like you and Carter here that panic like a couple of soft lasses."

Jonnie looked at Annie, those pale blue eyes cold in the flickering candlelight. "I'll deal with you later," Jonnie replied darkly.

Turning to Tim, she bent low: "Get out of here, mate, soon as you can, it's not safe; get out and wait for us in the cave."

"But what about me dad? What about our Jo?"

"Find them, tell them what's happened, but whatever you do, get out of here – I've got a feeling we won't have long." With that, she disappeared into the darkness.

Chapter 7

By the time she reached the cave, Daisy was filthy and exhausted. It seemed far less welcoming than it had during her storytelling sessions, with the warm fire and animated faces of the children. The only evidence remaining was a pile of ashes in the middle of the cave.

She suddenly realised how hungry she was: she hadn't eaten since early that morning and her stomach was rumbling. All that had been on her mind, since her argument with Annie, was escape. Now that she'd left Annie far behind, the reality of her situation started to hit home. What would happen now? She couldn't go home – Dad would be furious and ashamed, and Mam would cry. And Annie, Annie! She had it coming to her from Annie; Annie would tell Geordie and then what would happen? She knew she'd be no match against the two of them.

Her hunger started to disappear, replaced by a gnawing worry. What had she done? This wasn't new for Daisy – she'd always been hot-headed. Mam was always saying, "Daisy, pet, you think you can talk your way out of anything, but you'll learn." She remembered the time she got into trouble at Sunday school, when they'd been asked to draw a picture about Jesus feeding the five thousand. But it had been really warm that week, and all she wanted to do was play with her mates. Although she liked to learn, she would far rather be out in the fresh air, playing with her friends and making up stories, than sitting in that cold, musty-smelling church vestry. She wasn't all that sure about Jesus either: it all seemed very distant, about a man that was brought up a long way away, though the stories about how he died made her feel like crying.

She shivered. Her hair was still damp from the mine and her heavy woollen trousers were soaked through. Although lots of girls didn't wear any tops in the mine, she always wore an old shirt of her dad's, and this was soaked now too. Suddenly she felt desperate to be clean again, desperate to be free of the smell and filth of the pit. She rose and moved towards the entrance to the cave, and realised she had no idea what the time was. It was still light, and a thin, watery sunlight was just breaking through the clouds, transforming the sea from a dun, greyish colour to an inviting cobalt blue. Suddenly she couldn't bear it any more and, stripping off to her drawers, scampered headlong into the sea.

The cold hit her like an iron bar but, gasping with pain and shock, she waded out deeper, waiting for the moment when the pain would turn to numbness and the sea would embrace her like an old friend. Rubbing herself vigorously to get rid of the pit filth, she felt a calmness come over her. She could never go back there. She didn't know what she'd do, but she could never return to the darkness again. In the distance a lonely gull cried out from top of the cliffs, its cry breaking the silence. As she gazed in the direction of the sound, it spread its wings and took flight, soaring high above her, making for the thin violet line that marked the horizon. A single cloud blocked out the bright sunshine and Daisy shivered; the sea that had looked so welcoming only seconds earlier was now a steely grey as she waded back to the shore. Dusk would be falling soon; what would she do then?

* * *

Evie woke with a jolt. For a moment she thought she was back at the cottage, in her little cupboard; but Jonnie, where was Jonnie? It was the smell that reminded her where she was, that terrible smell like rotten cabbages and Charlie the pig all rolled into one.

Evie hadn't heard the rumble of a corve for a while now and she realised she'd been dreaming, dreaming of being in the sunlight with Jonnie: dreaming that her auntie and uncle were gone, and that it was just Jonnie and her, living together in the little house. Waking to the inky blackness, she began to cry. When would Jonnie come for her? Would he forget and leave her here all night, with the ghost of the Pit Wife? Or worse, would he try to find her and not be able to? Maybe that was what was happening now; maybe he was wandering the tunnels crying her name, lost for ever in the maze. She'd never find her way back to the top without him! Her sobs sounded deafening in the dark tunnel, but at least it was better than that terrible silence.

After a while her crying subsided, only to be replaced by a bad attack of the hiccups: "hick", the sound echoed in the tunnel, "hick", "hick". The hiccups were coming faster now and she started to try to count them. Unlike Jonnie, Evie loved the times that she attended Sunday school, and had even managed to pick up one or two numbers. She loved the bright pictures of the saints on the wall of the damp-smelling vestry, and listened intently to Mrs Thundertone recounting stories of Jesus and sins. She didn't really know what a SIN was, but she knew it was something bad, and that bad things would happen if you did a SIN. Mrs Thundertone's face would turn bright red and her normally shrill voice would boom with menace when she mentioned SIN.

"The SINS of the FATHER will be visited on the SON," boomed Mrs Thundertone, addressing herself to the ragged assortment of boys and girls in the room. But Jonnie and the other boys were unimpressed with Mrs Bright's dramatic performance, and her booming voice was met with yawns and the odd scratching sound; Jason Veitch even had the cheek to be picking his nose.

"And YE shalt not pick thy NOSE in a public place, or it SHALL get sore and FALL off." This particular saying stuck in Evie's mind, and she imagined the day when Jason Veitch's nose would fall right off, in the middle of Sunday school. The thought was so astounding that, for a couple of seconds, it even held the hiccups at bay and for a minute silence reigned in the dark tunnel.

"BOOM." Evie jumped, hitting her head against the low ceiling. "BOOM." The noise resounded again in the tunnel, and she trembled as the ground shook beneath her. This time, a shower of small stones rained down on her from the roof above.

She froze, her eyes fixed on the trap door in front of her. Any minute now she expected the Pit Wife to emerge from the tunnel beyond, her booming footsteps announcing her arrival. There was only one thing she could do and, gathering her sopping skirts to her, she began to crawl away from the door, back in the direction she had come from that morning, back to the only person who would keep her safe; back to her Jonnie.

* * *

Ever since she was little, Jonnie had known things, things that others didn't. Her mam said it came from her side of the family and would tell Jonnie stories about her life when she was young; how she and her own mam, her dad and her three sisters had travelled around: her dad making money from training horses;

her mum from selling her beautiful hand-made lace and by telling the fortune of the women who came to her. Jonnie loved the dark winter nights when they would all sit in the cosy front room, Evie sleeping soundly in the cradle beside the roaring fire, and their dad snoozing contentedly in the armchair draped with lace cloths made by her grandmother. Sometimes on those evenings one of the local women would knock on the door, begging Mum to use her gifts to look into the future and see what was in store. On these nights Josephine would leave the warm fireside and make her way across the dark yard to her little fortune-telling hut. As Jonnie grew up, her mum allowed her to watch her at her work, and soon she too came to understand how to read the beautiful pictures on the brightly painted cards, and to make out the pictures that appeared in the tea leaves, right at the bottom of the cups when the women had finished drinking tea. She learned how to handle her mother's collection of beautiful crystals that glittered and shone by the light of the candle. The only thing that Jonnie wasn't allowed to touch was her mother's collection of crystal balls, two transparent, and one coal-black crystal that sat on its own stand surrounded by candles.

"Why can't I touch the crystals?" she'd asked. "You let me help with other things and learn how to read the signs, but you'll never let me look into the crystals."

"Only older fortune tellers can look into the crystals," she replied.

"But why?"

Josephine sighed. "Sometimes you see things in there, things you might not be able to control. Perhaps soon I'll let you have a go of the white crystal. It's kinder and its messages are softer. But you must promise me never, ever to look into the black one."

Jonnie shuddered. The black crystal stood at the far end of the room, covered by a thin piece of black silk.

"I promise, cross my heart."

She should have known what was going to happen. She could have saved them if she'd acted on her feelings, but she hadn't, and that's why Mum and Dad had died; it was her fault for ignoring the signs. She'd been playing, in the usual place on the green, across from the common. Evie was running around on the grass, giggling and laughing, and she was lying on her back, looking up at the clouds. Suddenly a shadow fell across the sun. The other children carried on playing, their laughing cries fading as she dozed off. Suddenly she woke with a jolt, her eyes springing open. The clouds above her seemed to be changing shape, swirling and dancing around the fading sun as she stared, a flock of birds appeared from nowhere, flying so low that you could even hear the swishing and flapping of their wings. At the same time, a terrible odour filled her nostrils: a burning smell. Choking, she jumped to her feet, rushing over to where the younger children were playing. "Take cover, quick!" she screamed. Gathering Evie in her arms, she began to run towards the cover of the old elm tree. White with fear, they all crouched under the lowest branches while the birds circled around. Then, as suddenly as they'd arrived, they disappeared, the swish, swish of their wings ringing in the children's ears. Emerging from the protective skirts of the tree, the children could just make out the dark outline of the flock, disappearing into the distance.

"They're making for the mine," said a little voice, beside her. Jonnie nodded, squinting in the bright sunlight as she gazed in the direction of the dark wheel that loomed over the main shaft. The other children soon lost interest in the birds and resumed their game of tag. But Jonnie continued to stare in the direction of the mine, mesmerised by the black cloud that was forming in the air over the pit wheel. Was she imagining it, or were the birds forming a shape in the air? Just then a distant siren marked the end of the shift and the pit wheel slowly began to turn; at the same time, the birds began to swirl around the wheel until the sky above the pit began to look like a giant black whirlpool. She should have known then that this was a sign. But instead she ignored the terrible feeling in the pit of her stomach, and kept the warning to herself.

Her eyes filled with tears as she remembered the last glimpse she'd had of her dad: tall and lean, with his blond hair and piercing blue eyes, waving her goodbye as he set off for his thirteen-hour shift in the dark. Like Jonnie, he was sensitive and artistic; it had been a real surprise to everyone when he had taken a job at the mine. But in many ways, despite his soft looks and ready smile, he was a brave man: it had taken some guts for him to marry Josephine, a Gypsy, when so many of the villagers looked down on the Gypsy folk as being dirty, thieving rogues. At first the villagers made fun of him working down the pit:

"He'll never survive, a willowy chap like him."

"Give him a couple of days and he'll be out of there."

But William showed them what he was made of, and before long he'd earned respect among the pit folk, and his missus with him.

And now Jonnie felt it again: that terrible feeling deep in the pit of his stomach. There was going to be trouble – big trouble – and all she could think of was getting Evie and herself out of the pit: out of here and away from this place for ever.

Chapter 8

Jonnie had just reached the point in Skry Pit that they called the Bridge (it wasn't a real bridge, but a crossroads where four of the main pit passages joined each other), when the force of the explosion knocked her off her feet, throwing her against the walls of the tunnel. Dazed by the blow, she lay there for what seemed like ages. It was the smell that brought her to her senses; that terrible smell of rotten eggs. Groping her way upright, she strained to see what lay ahead. The smell was getting stronger by the minute. Door four, she had to get to door four to fetch Evie before it was too late. She froze in the darkness as a dark shape appeared out of nowhere: was this one of the mine ghosts, come to warn her again? With a gentle snicker, the pit pony looked up from his manger, a piece of straw hanging from the corner of his mouth. Jonnie sighed with relief and gave the creature a comforting pat on his warm back, resting her forehead for a minute against the warm comforting flank. Sighing heavily, she shook her head in despair: how would she ever find Evie in this maze of tunnels? She couldn't even remember coming this way, so she must have taken a wrong turn somewhere. Her hands shook as she continued to stroke the pony. Not used to this kind treatment, the animal gave another soft whinny and turned its blinkered head towards Jonnie, nuzzling her with a wet nose.

"I'll never find her," she whispered. "I'll lose her like I lost Mum and Dad." The pony whinnied again and gave her a nudge towards the tunnel.

"What you saying, boy?" demanded Jonnie. "What you telling me, mate?"

The pony nuzzled her again, this time a little less gently.

"You telling me to go on, mate? Is that what you're telling me?"

The animal whinnied and this time stepped away from her. Stepping back from the stall, she took a deep breath.

"Lead on then mate," she urged, as the pony trotted into the blackness.

Before long, they arrived at another trap door. The roof of the tunnel was higher here, so she and the pony were able to pass easily through the trap door. The rope that should have opened it was hanging limply from the wall, but there was no sign of the trappy lass or lad. Pulling hard on the rope, the door creaked open, giving way to a narrow passage. As they continued she was aware that the ground underneath them was sloping quite steeply now, which must mean that they were heading in the direction of the surface. She knew that the main shaft wasn't the only entrance to the tunnels: there was a day hole set into the hillside that could be used if the cage failed. Pausing for breath, she heard the ominous clanking of a corve, not near yet but definitely coming closer. Desperate not to be seen, she felt anxiously around the tunnel walls for somewhere to hide. The clanking drew closer and the sweat rolled down her back. She could hear voices now and, stumbling back towards the door, she felt for the rope. No time, there was no time; in desperation she flattened herself in the small space just in front of the door, as the pit pony forged on ahead.

Jo's head was killing him. He could barely see now, the pain was so bad. Straining to push the heavy corve through the door, he barely noticed the figure crouched on the other side.

"Push harder, you useless object," shouted Geordie Giles, as he strained to pull the heavy corve through the door, his head down and the heavy leather belt straining around his thick waist. Jonnie flattened himself against the wall, hardly daring to breathe.

"Well, well, well, what have we here then?"

Jonnie froze, but Geordie Giles had passed his hiding place and seemed to be talking to someone further down the passage.

"A little Wear, eh? Well now, little Wear, where do you think you're off to? Off to find soft big brother, are we?" he laughed.

Evie cowered by the side of the track.

"Leave her be, Giles, she's only a bairn."

"Well, it seems that the bairn isn't doing her job, eh? What's she doing – searching for Mam and Dad, are we? Or maybe for big brother." His face darkened. "Well, not if I find him first. Now maybe she'll lead me to him, eh, how about that, eh?"

"We'd better take you with us then, eh, pet. You'd be better than old Jo behind there. Mebbies I'll take the chain and belt off Jo, and put it around your little waist, that'd be a laugh. Oh, it would be grand to see old Jonnie's face when he cops a load of you pushing this thing," Giles cackled.

Just as Geordie bent to make a grab for Evie he caught sight of the dark shape ahead. By the weak light of the candle the pony looked like a ghostly giant in the gloom. As Geordie hesitated, Jonnie stepped out of the shadows, right into his path.

"Forget it, Geordie", said Jonnie, stepping out from the shadows. "You leave her be: whipped you once today; happy to do it again."

"Oh aye, Wear, a fight down here would be a bit different, eh? See, I've got something that would even up the score." By the weak light of the candle, Jonnie caught the glint of a blade.

"Drop it, Geordie," ordered Jonnie, trying not to show her fear.

"Oh aye, and who's gonna make me?" said Geordie, taking a step towards Evie. "Let's see what this does to her pretty face."

Jonnie lurched forward but in the same second a large lump of coal caught Geordie on the back of the head and he fell forward with a groan. Jo emerged from the back of the corve.

"Just go now! He'll wake up in a minute – that won't keep Geordie down for long. You'd better get out of here, and quick," he said, rubbing his swollen temple.

Jonnie rushed forward and embraced the boy. "Jo," shouted Jonnie with almost crying with relief. "You saved my Evie, we can't leave you down here to face that," she said, pointing at Geordie, slumped on the ground.

"Why've you both left your doors, Jonnie? Bri will kill you when he finds out."

"It's a long story, mate," said Jonnie, grimly. "A long story. Come with us and I'll tell you on the way."

"No, mate," said Jo, sadly. "Me dad already thinks I'm a coward. I been off sick all last week; I can't leave now."

"You have to," urged Jonnie. "This place isn't safe. Too many of us have left our doors now; the gases'll blow soon."

"Plenty have left doors before and nothing happened," countered Jo. "Why should it be any different this time?"

Jonnie grimaced in despair. How could she explain how she felt? It would just sound stupid for a lad to talk about feelings.

Meanwhile, unnoticed by the pair, Evie had taken herself off a little further down the passage and was stroking the pit pony.

"Jonnie, come and look at pony," shouted Evie.

Jo unchained himself from the corve and he and Jonnie moved towards the sound, smiling as they caught sight of Evie crouched beside the pit pony, her face beaming in the candlelight.

"Someone's happy," grinned Jo, for the first time that day.

Jonnie was just about to reply when she caught sight of something hanging in a dim corner of the stall. She'd not noticed it before but now, on closer inspection, it looked like some sort of cage. Turning to Jo, she pointed to the thing.

"What's that, mate?"

"Oh, that'll be old Connie," grinned Jo. "Our little singer."

Jonnie looked puzzled, "Connie?"

"Yeah, the old mine canary. They keep them down here in the mines. The old boys like the singing and 'course they're useful as well."

"Useful, how do you mean?"

"Well, they sing, don't they, but they only like fresh air, so when they stop singing you need to be careful. Like as not they've smelt bad gases, so they stop," said Jo, sagely.

Jonnie moved gingerly towards the cage, straining for a sight of the bird. By the side of the stall a candle was stuck on the ridge of rock and, taking a match from her pocket, she lit it. In a second, the whole stall was illuminated by the tiny candle. Moving closer to the cage, Jonnie, Jo and Evie peered inside.

The yellow bird lay on the bottom of the cage, its beak open as if singing. But this little tweeter had sung its last song; it lay stone dead, its claws curled, its feathers smooth and perfect.

Jo turned to Jonnie anxiously. "Looks like you were right, then. It's a goner, which must mean that there are gases around here somewhere," he said, scanning the roof, as if he expected to see something. "We need to find Dad and tell him so he can evacuate the mine."

"No time," replied Jonnie, "and, anyway, your Tim's gone to do that."

"What about me sister, though!" Jo shouted, his voice croaky with fear.

"Don't worry about her. She's gone, up to the cave on the beach. Come on now, we've got to get out of here, time's running out," urged Jonnie.

Jo blanched with fear.

"Come on, then, I know how to get out by the day hole, the passage through the hillside. It comes out just the other side of the hill, the side that faces towards the sea," he urged.

Grabbing Evie's hand, Jonnie tore her away from the pony and dragged her along the passageway. Jo was in the lead: he knew the old mine like the back of his hand and confidently led the way towards the day hole.

"I want pony," wailed Evie. "I want the pony."

"We can't take him, we can't," pleaded Jonnie. But Evie wasn't having any of it and stubbornly refused to move.

"Grab his harness, we can take him as far as the day hole. He'll be all right from there," whispered Jo. "She ain't going to move without him."

Grimly, Jonnie nodded and, fumbling with the thick rope, the trio began to climb the slope that led to the surface.

Chapter 9

Jay was furious. Sweat mixed with coal dust and ran down his face in rivulets.

"I cannot understand what she's playing at," he boomed as Tim cowered beside him. "Leaving the corve and then you, leaving the door," he shouted, pushing his face into Tim's.

"But Da, you don't understand, it was Annie's fault. She was the one that made Daisy bad; it was her."

Wiping his brow with the back of his arm, Jay stood, his pickaxe in one hand, the other holding up the midgy lamp, which illuminated Tim's anxious face in the dark. "If this is all true, then I've got no choice. I'll have to tell Bri. One door and we could all blow."

The other miners shook their heads in disgust. "It's not like your Daisy, mate. It's a bad business, though, all the same, putting us all in danger like that."

Jay grimaced. "Aye, it was my family got us into this mess, so it'll be my family that gets us out." Kneeling down, he whispered in Tim's ear: "You get out of here and leave me to sound the alarm. I'll follow you up, soon as I've let everyone know."

"No, Da, I'm not leaving you," Tim cried, hot tears running down his cheeks.

"Just do it," boomed Jay. "There's no time to waste. Take passage number one: that leads to the day hole. That way, if anything does happen to the main shaft, you'll still be able to get out." And with that, he disappeared down the passage to fetch Bri.

* * *

Blinking in the bright sunlight, Jonnie, Jo and Evie made a strange crew, standing on the hillside: Jonnie filthy and still bruised from the morning's fight; Jo chalk-white, his head swollen and sore; and Evie, dirty and wet, her curls hanging limply to her shoulders.

Jonnie breathed at last and, with him leading the way, the crew descended to the beach.

Tim was out of breath when he reached the cave. Just inside the door, Daisy was waiting anxiously for him.

"Oh Tim, Tim," she cried, throwing her arms around him. "I thought you'd never come. I thought I'd killed you," she whispered dramatically.

Tim turned to her. "We're not out of the woods yet. Dad and Jo are still down there. Jonnie and Evie too," he added sadly.

Daisy chewed her lip anxiously. "But they will get out, won't they? I mean, they won't be stuck down there for ever?"

"Let's hope not, Daisy," Tim sighed wearily. "Let's hope not."

It was nearly dark by the time Jonnie, Jo and Evie reached the cave. Exhausted with crying, Evie fell asleep almost immediately, while Jonnie and Jo set about making a fire, all the while recounting the tale of Geordie Giles.

"What about Dad," cried Daisy. "I'm so worried about Dad."

Tim and Jonnie exchanged glances, neither wanting to say what was on their mind.

"Dad'll be all right," said Tim, sounding more confident than he felt. "He knows that mine like the back of his hand. He'll be fine," he said, turning away so she couldn't see the terrible guilt and pain on his face. What if Dad wasn't all right? What if he didn't get out in time? The thought was almost too much to bear.

The five of them sat in silence, huddled around the tiny fire that Jonnie and Jo had managed to make out of driftwood.

"We'll wait until we hear the siren go, then we'll go and see what's what," announced Jonnie decisively.

"It'll be the worst thing ever," cried Daisy. "I can't go back, not even for Mam and Dad. And what about when they find out what

Jo did to Geordie? If Annie doesn't kill him, her mum certainly will."

"Shut up, Daisy," shouted Tim, his upset turning to anger. "It's all your fault anyway; none of this would have happened if it weren't for you."

"That's so unfair," she countered. "How can you say that after the fights you and Jonnie had with Geordie this morning?"

Tim looked broodily into the fire. He needed to blame someone, needed to get angry to stop these terrible thoughts coming into his mind.

Jonnie looked into the flames. She knew in her heart of hearts that she couldn't ever return down the mine: she couldn't put little Evie through all of that again. Glancing over at her sleeping, she felt a sinking feeling in the pit of her stomach. How would she look after her? Keep her safe? They couldn't stay here or their aunt and uncle would force them back down the pit again. Staring at the bright colours, her eyes clouded over. Something was in there, in the fire; it was happening again, that feeling, it was getting stronger. Squinting with the heat, she stared deep into the flames. As she gazed, she could make out what looked like a street; not a street in Skry but a street with lots of tall buildings. As she stared, a figure appeared out of the doorway of one of the buildings and turned to face her. It was her, an older her, and there beside her was a young woman who looked very like Evie. A fat woman with a basket suddenly appeared in the picture.

"Welcome to London," said the woman, shaking her hand. "You took your time getting here." Jonnie drew back; the face looked familiar but she couldn't remember where or when she'd seen the woman. Peering closer, she felt the flames lick at her face.

"Jonnie, what you doing, mate! You'll singe your hair off," shouted Jo in alarm.

Jonnie drew back, the smell of singeing hair in her nostrils. It was another sign, she knew it, just like the ones Mum used to have.

"We're going to London, that's it decided," she said, looking up at them. "You coming or you staying?"

Tim looked incredulously at her. "You're mad, mate. What brought that on?"

"We're going and that's that. There's no future for me and Evie here any more, so I'm taking her to London."

In the silence that followed, Daisy looked over at Tim, before slowly getting to her feet. "I'm coming 'n all, Jonnie. I want to come with you."

"What are you talking about!" shouted Tim, seizing her by the arm. "What about Mam and Dad? What about me and the rest of them back there?" he shouted in her face.

"What about them? What about me? What sort of a life am I going to have from now on, once everyone finds out what I did? Me and Jo can go together; he hates his job as much as I do."

"But what about the money? How are Mam and Dad going to survive without your money?"

"We'll send it home to them, won't we, Jo? Soon as we're settled, we'll send it home. We can earn good money in London; I've heard about it. We'll be rich and we'll never have to go down the mine again."

Tim looked aghast. "You're mad! Jo, you're not going along with this, are you?"

Jo hesitated for a minute before replying. "She's right. What sort of a life do we have here? Every day in the pitch black: every day toiling away, no rest, no play, just pitch-black stinking toil from now until we die, of hard work or worse. I'm going to London with them," he finished.

Tim shuddered; this was madness, madness – but if they went, then what would he do? What would there be left for him?

They sat in silence, thinking about a future that none of them could contemplate.

It was the trembling they felt first; before the smoke, before anything else, it was the trembling.

"What was that?" said Jonnie.

"I felt it too," replied Daisy, looking anxiously at the roof of the cave where a few small stones had loosened and tumbled into the fire.

"There it is again."

This time, the trembling was too strong to ignore. It knocked tiny sticks from the fire and woke the sleeping Evie.

Tim rushed out of the cave with Jonnie hot on his heels.

"Look," he pointed, "smoke, smoke coming from Skry, masses of it. It's happened, Skry's blown up and we're all to blame," he screamed. "It's all our fault and Dad'll be dead and it'll be all our fault," he cried, tears pouring down his face.

The children rushed down to the beach where the view of the pit was much clearer. Sure enough a pall of thick black smoke floated above Skry Pit. Nearby, a flock of birds took flight, soaring high above the pit and heading off south, away from the smoke and noise. As they stood there another huge explosion rent the air; followed by deathly silence. No one was in any doubt anymore; Skry Pit had blown and it was all their fault.

Chapter 10

Nothing but the calling of a distant crow broke the silence that followed the last terrible explosion. The children stood there, their gaze riveted on the distant pit wheel and the pall of black smoke that now hung menacingly in the air above it. Suddenly they heard the crunch of footsteps on stones.

"Quick!" cried Jonnie. "Make for the cave."

The five of them rushed for the mouth of the cave. As he entered, Tim stumbled and, desperate to recover his balance, felt a heavy hand on his shoulder.

"Steady there, our Tim, steady." Tim turned to see Jay's mate Paddy standing with his two dogs, Beamer and Bonny.

"Paddy," croaked Tim. "You got out. Is Dad safe?" he demanded.

"That I can't say, lad," replied Paddy. "I was on the early shift so last I saw he was with Bri the Bank. I was well clear when it all went up." Tim's face fell in despair.

"Tim lad, I need to have a word with you and your mates," he said heavily.

As they entered the cave, they could see that Paddy was struggling to control his tears.

"I'm sorry for you, sorry for you all; it's not easy what I have to say now," he said awkwardly, trying desperately to find the right words. Taking a deep breath, he began: "See, the trouble is that, well I know you are supposed to be down there, I mean, down there now, and, em, well because you are all here, and like, I can see that you're all in a bit of a state, well, I think you know."

"You think we did it, don't you?" asked Jonnie accusingly.

"I don't know what to think," sighed Paddy heavily. "What I do know is that you're in trouble, just by the fact that you're here, I know that you must have something to do with all of this." He gestured, looking up at the roof.

"It wasn't us, Paddy," cried Daisy, wringing her hands. "It was Geordie and Annie Giles that are to blame," she added desperately.

"And where are they now?" replied Paddy.

The children looked at one another. Nobody spoke.

"I thought as much," sighed Paddy.

"You see, it doesn't really matter what you did. Because you are here, and they aren't, means that you'll get the blame. There's no telling what folk around here will do when they hear about it all. They won't be bothered about what really happened, all they will see is five kids that ran away from work and caused the biggest explosion this village has seen in a long time," he said sadly, shaking his head.

"So what do you think we should do, Paddy?" cried Tim anxiously, the tears now pouring down his face.

Before Paddy could reply, Jonnie interjected: "We're going."

"Going where?" demanded Paddy.

"London," replied Jonnie.

"London?" echoed Paddy. "That's a long old journey, that is," he said, scratching his head. "I've never been to London but I've heard about how it's a hard old place with strange people in it – foreigners they say."

"Yes, yes," said Jonnie, impatiently. "But lots of work, and the chance to get rich and never have to work down a pit again."

Paddy nodded slowly. "Aye well, that's something good lad, that's certainly something good."

"But what will we do for money? How will we get there?" asked Daisy, her tear-streaked face looking anxiously up at Paddy's.

"Well now, lass," replied Paddy, scratching his head. "Let me think on."

After what seemed ages, Paddy reached into his pocket and, producing a dirty leather pouch, handed it to Jonnie. "Here's enough to get you started, lad. I don't know how far it'll take you, but it's a start at least."

He shook his head again. He very much doubted that Jay and Bri would have survived the explosions; one, maybe, but not three. And now what was he doing? Like as not he was sending this lot to their death. Oh, maybe the blond boy would survive; he'd heard he could handle himself. But Tim, and Daisy? Too innocent, too sheltered by loving parents. And Jo? Well, you only had to look at the boy to see that his days were numbered; so pale, and that head looked badly infected. But it was the little one that pained him most: Evie, her thumb in her mouth, barely five years old. What would life on the road be like for her?

Still – he thought, shrugging his shoulders – there was no choice. It was this or nothing.

"I want to give you something else before you go. Something that will guard you on the road to London, keep you safe."

The children waited with bated breath; what could he be going to give them?

Nodding at Beamer, Paddy handed the string leash over to Tim. "Take Beamer, he's strong and he don't take kindly to strangers. He'll be the best protection you could have against thieves and robbers."

Beamer (so called because he always looked as if he was smiling) jumped forward and gave Tim a lick, as if to say, "I'm yours now, mate."

Tim smiled sadly. "Don't worry, Paddy. We'll take care of him if he takes care of us," he finished, solemnly.

"Right now, I'll take you to the road to London and set you off safe," said Paddy, moving to the entrance to the cave.

The children followed him off the beach and across the fields, skirting the village of Skry. The road to London was just beyond the village, but Paddy was careful to take them the long way round, so no one would know their plans, or suspect that Paddy had helped them to escape.

Suddenly Jonnie stopped short in her tracks. "I need to go and get something from the cottage. I can't leave without it," she said firmly.

"No way, mate," replied Tim. "Too risky."

"Please! It's all me and Evie have left of our mum and dad; I need to get it."

Tim and Paddy exchanged glances. It was very risky but, on the other hand, Jonnie's cottage was well outside of the village, and would be less risky than going right into Skry.

"Ten minutes you have, lad," said Paddy. "Ten minutes. We'll meet you at Hecate Cross, the crossroads just beside the old gibbet."

Nodding in agreement, Jonnie turned to Evie. "Stay here with Daisy, I'll be back before you know it." Evie started to cling but Daisy stepped in quickly, taking the younger girl by the hand.

"Come on, Evie, let's you and me take Beamer for a little stroll shall we?" Evie turned to look at the dog and, when she turned back, Jonnie had gone.

It was dark in the cottage, dark and smelly. A loud snore made her jump. In the chair, her aunt was slumped over, bottle in her hand. Tiptoeing past her, she made her way out to the yard, through the back door and out into the garden. Charlie the pig approached her, hoping to be fed; squeezing past his hairy hide, she made for the darkest recesses of his stall. There in a canvas bag, hidden beneath the filthy straw, were her mother's things; her crystals, her cards, and, most precious of all, the black ball, all wrapped in the colourful shawls she'd kept as a last reminder of her travelling days. Trying to stop herself retching from the overpowering smell of pig poo, she quickly let herself out of the stall.

"Is that you, Tom?" shouted her aunt, as she heaved her bulk out of the chair and into the yard. Jonnie froze. "Did you get the meat for tonight?" she called, emerging from the back gate.

"What are you doing back here?" she exclaimed, her eyes narrowing. "And what's that you've got in your hand?"

Her lips pursed, she loped unsteadily towards her. "You been thieving, then? Out thieving; like your thieving mother when you're supposed to be down the mine?"

"It's just some bits and pieces I forgot today, nothing important." Jonnie tried to duck around her but she stood firm, her enormous bulk blocking her path.

Grabbing Jonnie by the shoulder, she pushed her face into hers: "I said, give it here, lad." Panicking now – the day's events were catching up with her – Jonnie gave the older woman a massive shove.

Her aunt, unsteady on her feet with the alcohol, missed her footing and tumbled to the ground. Before she knew it, Charlie the pig was on her, sniffing around to see if he could find any titbits in her pockets. Barely turning to look back, Jonnie made her escape, leaving her aunt cursing and writhing in the mud.

"Get off me, you big fat lump of lard," she shouted at Charlie. But the pig, undeterred, carried on snuffling, pinning the squealing woman to the ground.

That'll teach her, thought Jonnie with a smile, as she leapt over the garden gate and disappeared in the direction of the crossroads.

The children were getting edgy by the time she returned.

"What a relief, mate," said Tim. "We thought for a minute that something had happened."

"Naw, all went fine, didn't see anyone at all," lied Jonnie.

"Well, this is goodbye then," said Paddy, a tear in his eye. "Take it steady and always keep together. You must keep together."

"We'll manage," said Jonnie, sounding a lot more confident than she felt. She betted that Paddy wouldn't be so keen to let them go if he'd known he was leaving them in the care of a girl, and not a big strong lad.

"Will you tell Mam that we're all right," said Daisy, sobbing.

"Tell her, when we get to London, we'll send money," said Tim, bravely.

"And that we're sorry for everything," he added.

Nodding slowly, Paddy turned to Jonnie. "You are the oldest lad here, so I'm looking to you to keep them safe. Here's something that might help you to do that, but don't open the bag unless things get really bad." Paddy handed Jonnie a haversack. Clutching the haversack, and holding Beamer firmly by the rope, she shook hands with the man. "I'll not let you down, sir. You can count on me."

Paddy watched them disappear into the distance. It was growing dark now, and cold. The only sound at Hecate Cross was the rustling of elm leaves and Bonny's pitiful whining, as she cried at having been parted from her lifelong friend Beamer. Paddy paused and watched them until they disappeared over the horizon, before finally turning for home.

Chapter 11

The four travelled in silence broken only by Evie's sobs.

"I'm so hungry," she wailed.

"Shh, Evie, I've got something here to eat."

"Where did you get that from?" enquired Tim.

"Snatched it from Auntie's. She won't be needing it for a while," added Jonnie. "She's where she belongs at the moment," she added with a grin, thinking of her lying in the mud, Charlie the pig snuffling away at her: that would teach her for all the awful things she'd done to the two of them.

"Where we going to sleep, Jonnie?" demanded Evie.

Jonnie bit her lip nervously; it would be dark in an hour or so and they had to find somewhere fast.

Daisy was crying again, thinking about her dad.

Tim gulped back his tears and patted her on the back. "Hush now, I got a feeling it'll be all right. Dad's a survivor, you'll see."

Jonnie cast a furtive glance at Jo, who'd been silent up until now. In the grey half-light he looked sicker than ever; his pale skin waxy yellow and the wound on his head looking infected.

Jonnie pursed her lips; if it wasn't enough to have Evie to look after, she now seemed to have the whole lot of them. This wasn't what she'd envisaged when she'd first thought of leaving. She'd imagined running away to freedom, just her and Evie. Now she had a sick boy, and a couple of kids who had never ventured further than their own village. How on earth was she going to take care of everyone on this massive journey?

They'd been walking for nearly three hours now, only stopping briefly to consume the meagre rations that Jonnie had managed to forage from her auntie's house. All of them were showing signs of exhaustion. Even the irrepressible Daisy looked down in the mouth. As they rounded a bend in the road, they spotted a hump-backed bridge.

"Water," croaked Jo, picking up speed and running towards the little river.

Lowering his head to the dark waters, he began to drink. Catching up with his brother, Tim lowered his cupped hands to the water.

"I have to sleep, Tim," said Jo, his thirst slaked, at least for the moment.

Tim studied Jo. He too had noticed Jo's colour and the bruising wound on his head, which looked sorer than ever.

"Don't worry, mate, we'll get sorted soon."

"We are sorted," corrected Jonnie, approaching the two boys.

"See, there's a haystack over there, well off the beaten track. We can cosy down there for the night."

In their exhaustion, the children had all but forgotten about Beamer, but now they started to giggle as the dog emerged from the icy waters, and shook himself vigorously, tiny droplets of water spraying the three of them.

"Howay, Beamer boy," said Jonnie, pushing the animal away affectionately. "I don't want a bath yet!"

The haystack was still warm from the afternoon sun, and the children were asleep in minutes. Evie cuddled up against Jonnie, while the others made little indentations in the sweet-smelling hay. Only Jonnie remained awake, staring at the sky above her. The moon, a golden crescent, was at its newest, a clean slim tear in a great black star-studded cloth. Feeling into the hessian bag, she pulled out the obsidian ball. Its blackness reflected the bright moon. Surely her promise didn't hold now that Mum wasn't here anymore. The ball seemed to beckon her, sucking her deep into its depths. Staring into it, she strained to see what was in store for them. But the ball remained black. Far in the distance, the cry of a hunting owl rent the air. Beside her, Evie stirred, her thick black lashes fluttering slightly as she dreamed. At her feet, Beamer lay curled into a ball, dreaming of being back on the beach, chasing seagulls and playing with his master. Finally, as the grey dawn crept over the horizon, she slept.

* * *

Annie stopped for a minute, winded, as she finally reached the day hole. It was pitch black and all around her she could hear the keening of women and the crying of children as they waited at the pit head. Behind her, Geordie coughed out the last effects of the gas, his face black with coal dust.

"We can't leave Mam down there, Geordie, we just can't do it," said Annie, pleadingly.

"What choice do we have? We don't even know if she's alive or dead, and you saw for yourself that the entrance to her passage was completely blocked. If she's alive, then they'll get her out. If she's dead, well ...." He paused, as if fighting back the tears. Annie could hardly believe her eyes. Her big strong bully of a brother crying? Surely not?

"I'll get them," he growled, his tears turning to anger. "I'll get them for what they done to us."

"We can't go after them," said Annie. "You know where they've gone. If we go after them, we'll never find out if Mam's alive."

"You think that's going to stop me?" Giles laughed unpleasantly. "You've got another think coming, my lass. Oh no, I'm going after them and you're coming with me," he growled, getting to his feet.

Annie was powerless to resist and, sighing, she followed him, as she always did.

"What about money?" she asked anxiously.

"I got this from old Bri's pocket," he replied, producing a wedge of notes from the front of his shirt.

Annie gasped. It was more money than she'd ever seen in her life.

"W-what about Bri?" she stammered.

"Oh, he'll not be needing it where he's gone," replied Giles confidently. "Now let's go."

As the pair walked away from the exit to the mine, Annie caught sight of something being brought out of the mine in a big white sheet, and a foot hanging just below it. Gulping she turned away, suddenly furious with Tim and Daisy, she spat in the dirt, and ran to catch up with her brother. Unseen by Annie, a tall figure in the crowd watched as she left. Jessie, Tim, Daisy and Jo's mother stood slightly apart from the group, her remaining children at her feet; the tears rolling down her cheeks.

Chapter 12

Tim was dreaming again. This time he was standing at the entrance to the mine holding hands with his mam, waiting for news of his dad, when suddenly the main wheel began to turn, drawing up the cage from the depths of the earth. Rushing over to the banktop, he pushed the other men aside and entered the winding shed. It was cold, freezing cold, and he stood alone listening to the clanking and groaning as the lift rose to the surface. He stepped forward, pulling the iron grill to one side. But the lift was empty – or was it? Tim could just make out a tiny object, glittering in the corner. Hunkering down he stretched out his hand. A tiny wren glittered with a life of its own. Suddenly, there was a crash, and the iron grill smashed back into place, trapping Tim in the lift. Desperately he tried to pull it back again, but the lift began to descend. Screaming, and with tears pouring down his face now, Tim was thrown to the ground as the lift gained pace and he plunged into the depths of the mine.

The early morning sun was just starting to dry Tim's tear-stained face, leaving little silvery snail tracks of salt. Beamer, whose ears had pricked up at the sound of Tim's sobs, wagged his short tail and began to lick the salt off his damp cheeks.

He opened his eyes to see Jonnie standing proudly in front of him.

“Another bad dream, eh?” said Jonnie a sympathetic smile on her face. “Your mate will keep you safe, won’t you?” She smiled, patting Beamer’s broad back. “Hoy mate, no need to nosh into him,” laughed Jonnie, pulling the dog away. “Got breakfast for you here.” She grinned, producing a dead rabbit from behind her back.

“Where did you get that from?” enquired Tim.

“Caught it, mate. I’m a rabbit-catching expert,” laughed Jonnie. “My dad taught me,” she added proudly. “Every Sunday afternoon, off we’d go into the forest with the snares.”

“Yes, but bet you can’t gut them as well,” remarked Daisy, appearing from around the haystack. “Gutting’s women’s work, my mam always did that.”

“Yeah, well, I can do both,” replied Jonnie, turning away so she wouldn’t have to look her in the eye.

It was going to be very hard to keep her secret, with this crowd around her all the time. Someone was bound to suspect sooner or later, especially now her body seemed to be changing.

“Anyone seen Jo?” she demanded worriedly.

“He was around the back of the stack when I last saw him,” replied Daisy. “Said it was more comfortable around there.”

Tim stood up, rubbing his back.

"Wouldn't want to spend another night on that," he said wryly, scratching his back. "I think there were more fleas in that than on old Beamer there."

Jonnie grinned. "Come on, mate, we have to keep moving. Let's get something to eat, and we can be on our way."

Daisy and Evie appeared from the other side of the stack.

"I'm hungry, Jonnie," whined Evie.

Jonnie produced a large loaf of bread and chunk of ham from the canvas bag.

"Right, you lot, we'll have some of this, but remember, it'll have to last. Don't know that any of you lot can hunt, can you?" she said, with that curious crooked smile.

"Best get Jo, then," said Tim.

Jonnie got to her feet and made her way around the back of the stack. But there was no sign of the boy. The only sign he had ever been there was a slight dent in the straw.

"We got to get moving," said Jonnie, returning to the rest of the crew.

"We can't just leave without him," cried Daisy.

"Where could he have gone?" said Tim.

"Right, five minutes to look for him, then we're off. We can't afford to stay here any longer. Who knows who is on our trail?"

But, try as they might, they couldn't find any trace of Jo.

"Well, at least that means he's all right. Probably just chickened out and gone home," said Jonnie, secretly relieved that at least she wouldn't have a sick boy to cope with, along with everything else.

"We can't just leave him," pleaded Tim.

"We haven't," retorted Jonnie wryly. "Didn't you notice, he's the one that left us."

"He's right," added Daisy. "Jo'll have run back to Mam, same as always. He never really wanted to come with us."

"We could leave him a message," said Daisy, "telling him we've gone, so if he does come back he'll at least know we were thinking of him."

"Yes, but what," replied Jonnie.

"Something that he'll know is ours. What have we got that we can spare to leave behind?"

Suddenly Jonnie had an idea. "This buckle from the knapsack Paddy gave us, we don't need that. We can leave it here with a bit of Daisy's ribbon and, look ... we can make an arrow out of these stones. That way he'll know where we've gone."

Satisfied with their work, the children paused a minute to look at the stone arrow.

Suddenly the hairs at the back of Jonnie's neck started to prickle and a funny feeling started in her tummy.

"We have to go: go now!"

"Why the rush?" demanded Tim. "Surely just five more minutes, just to see if he comes back, won't hurt?"

"No, NOW," replied Jonnie, the feelings getting stronger.

And, scared by the look on her face, the children gathered up their belongings and returned to the road.

* * *

Jo wondered how long it would be before they missed him. He hadn't slept all night. The pain in his head was getting worse all the time, and now a thin trickle of pus rolled down his cheek.

He couldn't leave her, in the end. It didn't matter what had happened, he couldn't leave Mam. Whatever the others had done, that was their problem. He would go back and be with his mam and take the consequences. Even if that meant going down the mine again; it was worth it to be back with his beloved mam. And besides, if Dad had died, she would be all alone. She'd need a man about the house to help out with the younger ones.

He hardly noticed his surroundings, putting one foot in front of the other, his eyes on the ground, as he trudged back to Skry. He'd not been going long before he heard voices. Anxious not to be spotted, he ran off the road and dived for cover underneath a huge cedar tree, flattening himself against its broad trunk: his cheek blissfully cool against the wood.

"They've been this way," snarled Geordie, "I know it." Scanning the horizon, he narrowed his eyes. His arm was bad, very bad, where he'd hit it against the rock on the way out of the mine. Wincing with pain, he stopped in the middle of the road.

"You go and find water," he said, turning to Annie. "I need to get this clean, otherwise it'll get infected," he grimaced.

Annie nodded and ran on ahead.

Sighing, he leaned against the tree, closing his eyes for a minute. A little rest wouldn't harm. That lot would be so slow, especially with that kid Evie dragging along. It wouldn't take much for Annie and him to catch up with them.

Behind the tree, Jo hardly dared breathe, as Giles began to snore.

Sighing with relief, Jo began to edge out from behind the tree, when suddenly he felt a heavy hand on his shoulder.

"What have we here, then?" snarled Giles. "Ah yes, the weird one, isn't it: the mummy's boy. The stupid brother with the baldy head."

"Leave me be, Geordie, I just want to get back home."

"Home? Home? There isn't a home to call home any more, not after what your lot done. Killed my mam, you lot did, done for her. And now we'll do for you," growled Geordie, grabbing Jo and shaking him.

Jo struggled, but his thin frame was no match for Giles, and the shaking and fear was too much for him. Giles grunted as Jo went limp in his arms.

"Got it," shouted Annie. "There's a stream, just up ahead there," grinned Annie, bounding towards them.

Giles turned to her, and Annie came to halt, gasping when she saw the body hanging limply in Geordie's arms.

"It's not what you think," snarled Geordie.

"What have you done to him?" gasped Annie.

"He just went, just like that. One minute he was all right, the next – just like this," said Geordie, lowering Jo onto the ground.

"Is he, is he … dead?" trembled Annie.

"Naw, 'course not, he's still breathing, just fainted I think. Typical Carter coward. Find any water, then?"

"Yes, there's a stream just down back there. We should get some for him. We'll be in trouble if he dies."

"Who's gonna know?" replied the boy with a sneer.

"I'll get us some water, give a bit to him, maybe it'll bring him round," said Annie, making off in the direction of the stream.

The cold water hit Jo's forehead, but he managed to keep his eyes shut. He knew that his only chance of escape was to make them think he was unconscious or even dead. That way they might leave him alone.

"Come on, Geordie, we done our best, he's not coming round," hissed Annie. "Leave him, it's not him we're after."

"I'm gonna finish him off, else he'll tell on us," said Geordie, a rock held high above his head.

Annie was horrified; it was one thing to leave the lad unconscious, but another to actually kill him.

"Leave him be Geordie, he'll not tell on us, remember what a scaredy cat he is; and anyway who'll believe him after what he and his lot have done."

Geordie took one last look at Jo before turning away in disgust. He wouldn't last another night out here with no food and water. That wound on his head had turned bad. He wouldn't be shouting his mouth off about Geordie and Annie in a hurry.

"Come on then, let's get after the others. They can't have gone far."

It was almost nightfall when Jo woke, to someone breathing on his cheek and a damp nose nuzzling him gently. Opening his eyes, he froze as he looked into the eyes of the deer, its huge antlers scraping against the bark of the tree.

Holding his breath, he waited to see what the creature would do next. Suddenly a doe appeared from out of the woods and, giving Jo one last sniff, the pair moved silently back into the forest.

Jo felt strangely calm. His eyes closed again and the dark branches of the cedar tree wrapped their long shadows around him as he sank into the deepest sleep of his life.

Chapter 13

Five miles away, in the village of Skry, the villagers moved away from the pit head in little groups. Some weeping over the bodies of loved ones and some, like Jessie, forced to spend another night wondering if their husbands, wives and children were dead or alive.

Only the rescue team remained. Hunched over a small campfire, the five men warmed themselves with a hearty soup and glass of homemade ale.

“Well lads, another day tomorrow,” sighed Tommy.

“How many left down there now, you reckon?”

“Still twenty tallies not been accounted for,” replied Jim, supping his pint.

Tommy turned to Robin, a small man with a wizened face. “Reckon there’s any hope then, Rob? After all, you’ve been at a few of these things now.”

“Difficult to say, mate,” replied Robin, shaking his head. “Depends on how far along the main passage blew.”

“Women missing down there?”

"Yes, a getter called Martha. Hard-faced lass, by all accounts, but a woman all the same. Two kids 'n all."

"And old Jay, he hasn't turned up yet. Bad business, that."

"Aye," said Tom, pulling on his pip. "Mebbies it's best if he's gone, so he doesn't have to bear the shame that his kids have brought on him."

The men fell silent, each looking into the flames with his own thoughts. Sometimes death wasn't the worst thing that could happen to a man. No, to die honourably was better than living in shame.

* * *

"I can't take a single step more," groaned Daisy, sinking to the ground. "Me feet are killing, and I'm starving, and I'm thirsty, and we're nowhere near London yet."

"Jonnie, is it far to London then?" whispered Evie.

"Yes, it's far," replied Jonnie, staring into the distance.

"Will we be safe there?"

"Course we will," she replied firmly, striding ahead.

Tim's face furrowed with concern. He knew that Jonnie was lying; he could tell by the way he wouldn't look at his sister when he replied. His dad used to do that whenever one of them asked him a difficult question. Oh, he'd sound confident, but he would never actually look at them when he said it.

Catching up with Jonnie, Tim caught his sleeve. "We need to stop now, mate. Our Daisy can't go much further."

Jonnie smacked her lips with annoyance. "She's going to have to be a bit tougher than this or we'll have to leave her behind. We can't afford to lose time now, or the Skry lot'll catch up with us and put us away for what we did back there."

Tim looked anxiously back at Daisy. "She's hungry, and she's hurt. Annie gave her a right going over back there. She might be really hurt."

Jonnie looked back at where Daisy was half-sitting, half-lying, in the road.

"We need to stick together, mate. We already lost Jo; we can't afford to lose Daisy as well," replied Tim with a grimace.

Jonnie stopped momentarily. Why did she always end up having to be the responsible one? Why, for once in her life, couldn't she just do what she wanted, rather than having to think of everyone else? It had been bad enough being a girl, but it was starting to feel even harder having to act like a boy. Suddenly she was weary: weary of having to look after people, weary of having to be responsible for her little sister and now this lot. Glancing at Evie, who was now bending over the groaning Daisy, she sighed. "All right, let's stop for a while then."

Throwing herself down on the grass verge, she stared up at the sky. Her bag was much lighter now than when they began. They'd gone through most of the food that Paddy had given them, and the odd bits that she'd managed to take from her aunt, and all that was left were a couple of stottie cakes. It was too dangerous to go near any farmhouses: the Skry Pit lot would be after them by now, and who knows how fast they were catching up? They didn't have to slow down for a five-year-old and a moaning Daisy, who didn't seem to be able to go for more than ten minutes without throwing herself on the ground and trying to get everyone to feel sorry for her. Frustrated and angry, she got to her feet. "I'm going for a walk," she announced, making off across the field.

"I want to come too, Jonnie," said Evie, running after her.

"No, you stay here for once, I want to be by myself," she shouted, then, seeing tears spring to Evie's eyes, patted her head gently. "Daisy needs you to look after her. You stay put and I'll be back in a bit. I just need to see what's over that hill there. There may be somewhere I can get more food."

As she approached the top of the hill, she ran out of energy and slumped down on a rock. What had she done? How was this going to end? She could see for miles around. Evie, Tim and Daisy were just dots now, along with the few sheep and cows that dotted the landscape. How were they going to get to London? No transport, no food, no shelter. The nights were drawing in; soon it would be dark early and they'd have to seek cover somewhere.

As she sat there, pondering their fate, she suddenly felt a movement behind her. Before she had a chance to turn round, a sharp blow on the side of the head caught her and she fell to the ground.

"You all right there, raklo[4]?"

Jonnie tried to focus, but everything seemed to be swimming around. Holding her head, and squinting through half-closed eyes, she could only just make out a dark-haired figure bending over her. At first she wasn't sure if it was a boy or a girl. The face was so dirty and, though it was framed by a mass of long dark hair, the top hat confused her at first.

"Ina Boness," said the girl, holding out her hand, pleased to make your acquaintance like. Sorry about the bonce: I was after a rabbit and got you instead," she grinned. Jonnie took her hand, surprised at the firm shake.

---

[4] Non-Gypsy boy

"You'll be all right in a minute," said the girl. "It was the rabbit, I meant to get the rabbit but you got in the way," she said with a guilty grin, holding out the sling.

Jonnie felt her head, where a large lump had started to form.

"I pity the rabbit that this was meant for," Jonnie grinned wryly.

"What's your name, raklo?" demanded the girl.

"What's it to you, shey[5]?" retorted Jonnie.

"Hey, how'd you know my lingo, raklo?" she said in astonishment.

Jonnie grinned. "You give me some grub back at the vardo[6], and I'll tell you then."

"No, you tell me. You a Gypsy, then, like me? You don't look like one, blondie!"

Jonnie grinned back. "And you don't look like a girl in that top hat and all," she retorted, rising to her feet.

Suddenly a bout of dizziness overcame her. "Aw this head! You've killed me," she moaned, falling to the ground again.

---

[5] Girl

[6] Wagon or caravan

Laughing, Ina pulled her to her feet. "Oh, Romany boy, we'll put you back together again. Lean on me, it's not far to my vardo. Mam will put you right."

* * *

Daisy looked anxiously at Evie. The little girl seemed to be giving up; she was just lying there sucking her thumb, staring at the darkening sky.

"When's Jonnie coming back?" she whispered tearfully.

"He'll be back soon, don't you worry," comforted Tim.

"You seem very sure of him. What if he doesn't come back at all? What if someone from Skry's caught up with him? They might be taking him back there to face the music already," frowned Daisy.

Tim scowled. The only way he could carry on was to think of the future, and that meant a future with Jonnie leading them down to London and to safety.

"He said he'll be back, and I believe him. He'll look after us, he promised, his word is good."

"You mean like he looked after our Jo? Left him, somewhere back there, to be picked up by Annie and Geordie?" replied Daisy, her face contorted with anger. "Some friend he is, and now leaving little Evie, and she's on her last legs. I doubt she'll even last the night."

"Just shut up, will you Daisy, always the drama queen," shouted Tim. "See, you're scaring Evie."

Daisy was just about to launch into another speech, when she suddenly gasped, pointing at pinpricks of light making their way down the hillside towards them.

Sweeping Evie up in his arms, Tim broke into a run, with Daisy in hot pursuit.

"Quick, down here," he panted, falling into a hollow behind one of the oak trees.

Peeping out over the edge, they could just make out the lights, moving closer now, like a chain of tiny diamonds.

"Oh no," groaned Tim, as he saw a dark shape dart out from the bushes. "Beamer, here boy!"

But Beamer was hot on the scent of whoever was approaching and, like a good guard dog, set to barking at whoever was about to invade their camp.

Tim groaned. They were lost now – Beamer would give them away. He had to get hold of the dog, before the people came any closer. Stretching his arm over the edge of the hollow, the rope that served as a leash was almost within his grasp when, suddenly,

Beamer whined and took off in the direction of the lights, leaving the three children alone in their hollow.

The voices were coming closer now, and Tim could hear shouting and laughing. "There must be loads of them," whispered Daisy tearfully.

"There's still a chance that they won't see us. We're really well hidden down here. Just keep still and quiet, and they might just walk by," said Tim, sounding far more confident than he felt.

"Here, down here, the grass is flattened so they must be around somewhere," shouted a girl's voice.

"Loose the dog, that'll lead us to them."

Tim groaned. They had no chance if the people had Beamer and, sure enough, it wasn't long before a wet nose peered over the edge of the hollow, and Beamer's big smiley face peered down at them.

"Hello, hello, what have we here then?" A man in a large battered top hat peered down at them. "Looks like three rascals to me," he smiled. "These kids have anything to do with you, then?" he said, looking over his shoulder.

"Hey, that's no rascal down there," said a familiar voice. "That there's my sister."

"Jonnie," shrieked Evie, scrambling over the edge of the hollow, sobbing with relief.

As the rest of the group arrived in the hollow, Daisy and Tim hung back uncertainly.

"Meet the family," grinned Jonnie.

"Uncle Sid and Auntie Rosie, this my little sister, Evie and my mates Tim and Daisy."

A tall dark man, wearing one of the most beaten-up top hats Daisy had ever seen, stepped forward and gravely shook hands with all three. "A very fine niece I have here." He smiled gently, grasping Evie's small hand in his. "Oh and not forgetting, a very fine nephew too," he grinned, gesturing towards Jonnie. "What do you think, Rosie?"

The tiny woman, also wearing a beaten-up top hat, smiled delightedly at the tiny girl. "Oh the double of our Josephine," she smiled sadly, reaching out and stroking Evie's head. "God bless her soul."

"She would still be here with us if it wasn't for that gringo[7] she married," she added darkly.

"Come on, our Rosie," comforted the man. "Josephine made her choice and she was happy with it, and these two here are our

---

[7] Non-Gypsy

gift from her." He smiled, looking over at Jonnie.

"Aye, and look at them, out on the open road. No way of going back to their village, and us with enough mouths to feed," said Rosie, shaking her head worriedly.

"Come on, our Rosie, it'll all work out in the wash. Let's hear the story first, and then we can worry about the rest later."

* * *

It was warm and dry in the caravan, with its rich red carpets and curtains.

Daisy sniffed. "Not much room in here then for us, is there?"

Ina smiled at Jonnie. "There's a spare bed in Sid's vardo, you can have that one."

Then, turning coldly to Daisy, she gestured to a small tent by the campfire outside. "You and her can sleep there."

"Fine by me," retorted Daisy, storming out of the wagon.

"Bit of a temper, your friend, eh?" grinned Ina.

Jonnie grinned sympathetically. "Yes, she can be a bit of a handful at times."

Installed inside the tent, Daisy fumed. Outside, at the campfire, it wasn't difficult now to see Jonnie's Gypsy parentage:

it was written all over her face as the fire illuminated the high cheekbones and slanting eyes while she laughed at something Ina said. In the firelight it was amazing that anyone would take her for a boy.

"I'm hungry," whined Evie.

"Oh, not again child: be quiet," snapped Daisy, as she glared out of the tent at Jonnie and Ina laughing together.

"Will you not come and have some dinner with us?" Daisy looked up to see the dark-haired older lady with the beaten-up top hat leaning over the tent. Before Daisy knew what was happening, Evie had wriggled past her and grasped the woman's dirty hand in her small one.

"You must be very hungry, little one?"

"She's fine," retorted Daisy. "I've been looking after her. She always says she's hungry, but she's just trying to get attention," she added, looking darkly at Evie.

"Now then, I'm sure you've been like a good mother to her, but you must be hungry too: I bet you haven't had a hot meal since you left your mam?"

That was it for Daisy. She had tried so hard not to think of Mam and the rest of them back in Skry and, for a while, back there on the road, she'd been able to put them out of her mind.

Now in the warmth from the campfire, with this woman talking kindly to her, it was all too much. Her eyes filled with tears and she choked back a sob.

"There now," said Rosie, putting her arm around the girl. "You come with me, and let's have a nice bit of soup, and you can tell me all about your adventures."

* * *

Jonnie grinned. It was impossible to be with Ina for five minutes without laughing.

"What are you going to do from here, Jonnie?" enquired Ina.

Jonnie frowned. "We'll make for London like we planned. Like you said, you can drop us off as you pass through the city on your way to the hops."

"Why don't you come with us there? You could earn money, you'd be with us, safer than going onto the streets in London," shuddered Ina. "They don't like Gypsies in London. What if they take against you, stick you in the workhouse? They'll separate the both of you, and you'll never see her again. Mind you, that wouldn't be a bad thing with the other one," she added, nodding in Daisy's direction.

"Daisy's not so bad, she just takes a bit of getting used to," smiled Jonnie.

But when she thought of the workhouse, a shudder went down her spine. They had never seen one before, but they'd heard people talking about them: terrible places where whole families were separated and never saw each other again: worked almost to death with hardly anything to eat or drink. And the punishments … terrible beatings for anyone who stepped out of line. Ina was right, girls and boys were separated; some never saw each other again.

Jonnie shook her head. "The workhouse won't get us. I'll find a job, find somewhere for the four of us to live."

"What, you'll keep that lot?" said Ina, pointing to Tim, Daisy and Evie sitting quietly by the fire and enjoying their first proper meal for a while.

"Yes."

"But why?" exclaimed Ina incredulously.

"Cos I said I would," replied Jonnie firmly. "Anyway, Daisy's old enough to work. She can try to get into one of the big houses, you know, into service."

"And him?" said Ina, pointing to Tim.

"He'll get something, maybe work on a stall. Plenty of fruit and veg stalls in London, eh?"

"Go on, come with us to the hops. It's fun, and you can make a bit there before you go to London. That way, you'll at least have a bit of a start."

Jonnie smiled enigmatically. "Go on then, tell me about these hops."

* * *

Evie's eyes widened as she entered the caravan. All around her, rows and rows of patterned china sparkled in the glow of the candlelight, the rich dark wood showing off their brightly painted surfaces to perfection. At the far end of the wagon, rich red hangings were drawn back to reveal a bed adorned with a rich blue coverlet embroidered with multi-coloured silken threads.

"You like the vardo, eh?" grinned the strange-looking girl, her dark skin exotic-looking against the rich hangings.

"Course, you can't sleep in here, little 'un: us kids sleep out there."

Looking towards the open door, Evie could just make out the dark shape of a tent beside the roaring campfire.

"Come, little dark one," said the girl, holding out her hand. "You'll be cosy in there with your friends."

Evie took Ina's warm hand and followed her outside. Daisy's dark head poked out from the blanket that half-covered the entrance to the tent. Looking darkly at them both, she held out her hand. "Come here, Evie, you'll be safe here with me," she hissed, casting a quick glance around her at the row of faces that stared at her from beyond the campfire.

Although the inside of the tent was nowhere near as luxurious as the wagon, it was still warm and cosy, and a far cry from the damp hillside where they had waited for Jonnie to return.

Daisy bit her lip nervously.

"What's the matter, Daisy?" It was so unusual for Evie to speak that at first Daisy didn't know what to say. They had been so busy getting away from the mine, and worrying about what would happen next, that they hadn't really had a chance to get to know each other.

Turning to Evie, Daisy grimaced. "Gypsies, you don't trust them, so you stay close by me, or they'll steal you away."

"Why would they steal me?" demanded Evie.

"Cos that's what they does; didn't your mam tell you anything?"

"Mum's dead."

"Well, your auntie then?"

"No, she never said nothing about Gypsies," replied Evie solemnly.

Daisy sighed with exasperation. Why had she been landed with this baby? Where was Jonnie? Out enjoying himself by the campfire with that madam, no doubt.

As she peered through the opening, she felt the heat of the campfire intensify. An assortment of people were gathered around it: a man and woman of about her mam and dad's age, an group of children, and some women. Beamer had found a couple of Gypsy dogs and was fighting with them over what looked like a bone. Jonnie and Tim were sitting together, and between them sat the tall strange-looking Ina. Every now and then she would throw back her head laughing, a flicker of gold shining in her mouth.

"What's that?" asked Evie.

'That's the Gypsy tooth," said Daisy, sagely. "It means you can talk to dead people, that does."

Evie's eyes widened in alarm. "Talk to dead people? Are they all dead people then?"

Daisy raised her eyes in exasperation. "Not them, silly."

"Well, where are the dead people then?"

"In those wagons, that's where they are," whispered Daisy, darkly.

Evie cast a terrified glance towards the dark shadows beyond the campfire.

"Will we be safe then?"

"Oh yes, we'll be safe, as long as we stay away from that girl," she hissed, pointing in Ina's direction.

Suddenly Jonnie caught sight of the pair of them and beckoned to them, holding out a steaming hot drink. Evie made as if to go to her, but Daisy held her back, pulling her close.

"Remember the dead people?"

Jonnie shrugged her shoulders as she saw the pair of them retreat back into the tent.

"What's up?" asked Ina.

"I expect they're just tired, eh, Tim?"

Tim shrugged; he'd seen the way his sister looked at Ina and knew at once she was jealous of the way that the older girl seemed to be able to make Jonnie laugh. Daisy liked to be the centre of things, and this Ina, with her strange ways and glinty smile, seemed to have all of Jonnie's attention. Everyone seemed to want Jonnie to like them; he was just that type of boy thought Tim ruefully.

He stared deep into the campfire. The flames licking up around the black kettle reminded him of home. What would his mam be doing now? Had Jo made it home?

"Have some tea, gringo?" Tim turned to see a kindly dirty face under one of the biggest, most battered top hats he had ever seen.

"I'm Ma Boness, but you can call me Rosie. Now, take this hot brew, boy, you look all frozen through."

Tim took a tentative sip of the hot liquid.

"Go on man, it won't poison you," grinned the woman. "Heard stories about how we poison little boys then, have you?"

"Course not," muttered Tim, trying to avoid looking at the woman.

"Yer mam probably told you to keep away from us lot, eh? Bet you didn't know that Jonnie was one of us, though?"

Jonnie, a Gypsy? That couldn't be true, could it? Not with his blond hair and fair skin.

"Yes, my man, Jonnie's mam was my only sister. Never wanted to speak to her again after she went and married a gringo, so we lost touch for years. Then word got out about what had happened to her and her man, down that pit. I told her never to go into that black hole, warned her that for our kind it's the worst place to be. We need the fresh air, the blue skies and nature."

Tim looked up at the older woman. Her dirty kindly face was creased with sadness now.

She pointed towards a small man in a battered bowler hat, talking animatedly to Jonnie and Ina. "Me and Sid, we only found out last year. Course, soon as we could, we came looking for her babbies. We went to Skry and found out that they were living with his people. That dirty old woman and that bad-tempered man. We watched them for a while; they seemed settled to be living like gringos, so we camped up for a while. Then that explosion came."

"You've been following us all the while, then?" gasped Tim. "All the way from Skry?"

"Aye, all the way from Skry. Saw that pair that were following you and all. Nasty piece of work they are." She grimaced.

"What pair? What are you talking about?" exclaimed Tim.

"That great big lump of a lad and his sister; a skinny, mean-looking lass."

"Geordie Giles!" exclaimed Tim. "It's got to be him and Annie."

"Aye, well, whoever they were, they hurt the lad."

"No," moaned Tim. "Not Jo!"

"SHHH! You'll wake the littl'uns," hissed Rosie. "Yes, we saw him knocked down by that big bloke and his skinny sister. They left him for dead, but he wasn't dead. Any fool could see that."

"How did you know?"

"Well you can tell by the old ways."

"You mean, magic?" replied Tim tentatively, all of the old stories of the Gypsies coming back to him now.

"Aye , well, it might seem like magic to you folks, but to us it's just good sense." She grinned wryly.

"We knew he was alive because the deer came to him: the deer won't go near a dead thing, unless they want to eat it!" she laughed. "Yes, your lad wasn't dead, just dazed. He was hot, very hot. That wound on his head had turned nasty, so we made a poultice and left it on his head along with a drink of water and some bread. It didn't take long before he came round and went on his way."

Jo saved! It was almost too much for Tim to cope with. He was so relieved; it was the one good thing that had happened since the mine blew.

He gazed adoringly at Rosie.

"But what about Geordie and Annie?"

"They weren't bothered about your brother, too busy searching for you. But we slowed 'em up a bit. Gave them a little something to make them sleep a while – popped it into their water bucket when they were sleeping like babies. It'll take them a while to sleep that off. Anyway, my man, enough of our story; now you tell me yours; I reckon you owes me one now."

The campfire had burned low by the time Tim had finished his tale. The others had long gone into their tents and wagons, and only Tim and Rosie remained.

"So that's it, really. I killed me own dad, me and Daisy did, we both killed our own dad."

"No," said Rosie. "Whatever you did, you didn't do that. It was just what happened, that old mine could have blown any time. Besides, we don't know that he died, he may just have been trapped down there for a bit."

"That's what I try to think," nodded Tim. "I try to think that they are bringing him up and that I'll see him again, and that one day we can live together and be happy."

"Aye well, and that may be, but for the moment you've got to put yourselves first. If they really think you were to blame for the explosion, they could put you away for a long time, and that wouldn't help anyone, least of all your mam."

"No," agreed Tim, shaking his head sagely. "For the moment we can't go back."

"Aye, and you've got Jonnie, eh? Jonnie to take care of you all?"

"Yes, he's a great lad," nodded Tim.

"Mmm, yes, a great lad," agreed Rosie turning away. "It's a funny old thing though: you know in my head I always dreamed that my sister had two girls."

Tim grinned. "Well, you got that wrong, eh?"

"Aye," replied Rosie, staring thoughtfully at Jonnie. "Maybe I did and maybe I didn't."

Chapter 14

It seemed that they had been with Ina's family for ages, yet it was only a matter of weeks since they'd packed up camp and moved on with the Gypsies. They'd reluctantly parted company with the other wagons a few days before, when some of the menfolk had managed to get work on farms as they travelled south. Since then, they had been travelling alone with Ina, her mam and dad, and their three dogs: Jelly, Molly and Jet.

Daisy kept away from Ina most of the time, and slept in the little tent with Evie. The tent was fixed to the front of the wagon, so that at night it joined up and became a part of it. Making use of some spare tarpaulin and sticks, and with Sid's help, Jonnie had managed to make a little tent of her own, and so far no one seemed to suspect that she was a girl – though occasionally she had seen Rosie looking at her thoughtfully.

"What's up?" she'd dared to ask one day, when they were sitting outside the wagons, alone. Daisy had gone off to pick berries with Evie, and Sid and Ina were showing Tim how to carve apple wood into spoon shapes.

“Just looking at you and thinking how much you remind me of your mum when she was young. Same high cheekbones and wonderful blue eyes.”

Jonnie looked down, the colour rising to her cheeks.

‘She was beautiful, was your mum,” mused Rosie.

“Yeah well, I guess Evie will be beautiful like her too, when she gets a bit older,” Jonnie quickly retorted. “I look like my dad as well,” she whispered, barely daring to look Rosie in the eye.

“Of course you do, you being a boy and all,” nodded Rosie, knowingly.

Jonnie turned to smile at her and, as she turned towards her, the sunlight between the trees turned her blonde hair shades of red and gold. Rosie gasped; her suspicions confirmed: Jonnie was no boy, she was sure about that. So why on earth would she pretend to be one?

Turning away so that Jonnie couldn't see the expression on her face, Rosie took a deep breath. "Jonnie, I've been thinking, it's time you came in the wagon with us now, it's getting too risky having you camp out there all alone."

"No way," shouted Jonnie, springing to her feet. "I mean, er, I'm fine where I am."

"No, I mean, we're like family now, aren't we, I mean, proper family, so you should be in the wagon with us," Rosie persisted.

Jonnie shook her head adamantly. "No, you don't understand, I want my own space, all right? I spent too long cooped up in a cupboard with Evie to want to share with anyone again."

Rosie nodded, more convinced than ever that all of her instincts were right. Jonnie was a girl, but for some reason she didn't want anyone, not even her own sister, to know.

"All right then," she agreed, "have it your own way for now, but when we get to London we'll have to think again. The city's too dangerous for anyone to be sleeping on their own."

Jonnie nodded. At least that would give her a little bit more time.

Rosie walked back towards the van, shaking her head. What could have happened to make Jonnie want to be a boy? And how long could she keep up the act, when every day she was changing from a girl to a woman?

* * *

They had only been camped in the new camp for a night. They were close to London now. A few more days' travelling and they would reach the outskirts. The wagon was parked close to a stream, where old Bosher their horse could drink to her heart's content. It was a dull day, one of those days when the light began to fade early. The little group had decided to get an early start the next day, so that they would be in good time to get work picking hops in a place just the other side of the city. Jonnie was lying in her tent, listening to the hoot-hooting of the owls, when a terrible snarling and snapping came from the far side of the wagon.

Jumping out from beneath her blanket, she crawled out through the flap, just in time to see Sid disappearing into the woods. By that time the dogs were barking like mad, waking everyone up.

"What is it, what's going on?" whispered Daisy anxiously.

"Somebody was snooping around outside. The dogs were barking like mad so Sid went out to see what was happening. Next thing I knew, he was gone," said Rosie, worriedly.

"He must have followed them into the woods," said Jonnie. "I just caught sight of him disappearing. Do you think it's them?" she asked, turning to Rosie.

"Maybe, although I thought we must of lost them way back."

"Who are you talking about?" demanded Daisy.

Rosie and Jonnie exchanged anxious glances. Jonnie paused. "It could be Annie and Geordie. Rosie found out they'd been following us since Jo left."

"You should have told me that," shouted Daisy. "All you told us was that Jo was all right. Now you're telling us that he ran into Annie and Geordie?"

"All right, all right, keep your hair on," retorted Ina. "We knew you'd go off your rocker: that's why we didn't let on."

"Oh, you would know best, eh, madam? I expect you sucked up to Jonnie and concocted the plan together." Then, turning to Tim: "Did you know?" she demanded, giving him one of her most ferocious stares.

She didn't need a response to know that he did.

"Well that's great, thanks a lot."

"Daisy, be reasonable. What good would it have done to tell you? Jo got away and that's all that matters," Jonnie said, trying to smooth Daisy's ruffled feathers.

Daisy was just about to go into one of her great long tirades, when Tim interrupted.

"What does that matter now! We should be in there helping Sid. If it is Geordie and Annie in there, he's in real danger."

"He's right," nodded Ina. And before anyone could stop her, she turned tail and disappeared into the dark wood.

Chapter 15

"You'll have to go after her," pleaded Rosie. "She's so headstrong, there's no telling what she'll do."

Jonnie and Tim needed no further bidding and plunged into the forbidding darkness after her.

Suddenly Jonnie stopped in her tracks. "What's that noise?" she demanded.

"I hear it too," whispered Tim. "Sounds like something's coming this way."

"Maybe it's Sid," replied Jonnie, hopefully.

"Him or them," said Tim grimly, every muscle tensed for a fight.

As suddenly as she had left, Ina reappeared. Flushed from her run, her face was scratched and bleeding from the dense woodland.

"Why did you run off like that?" demanded Jonnie. "We've got enough on our plate with Sid to look for, without you going and worrying everybody."

"I wanted to help," pleaded Ina. "He's my dad after all." Jonnie was about to reply when Tim put his finger to his lips, motioning quiet.

"Listen."

As the three of them listened, a low moaning noise broke the silence.

The noise seemed to be coming from the far side of a pool of inky black water in the middle of the glade. As they carefully made their way to the far side of the pool, the moaning grew louder.

"What we going to do if it's them?" said Tim worriedly.

"Well, they don't sound as if they are fit to do much," replied Jonnie.

"Could be a plan just to get us back into the forest, then they'll strike," Ina said.

"She's right, Jonnie. I don't think we should all go together. If it is a plan then at least one of us should stop here, ready to go and get help. If it is Geordie and Annie they're bound to be armed."

Jonnie stopped in her tracks. "All right, well, Ina, you stop here while Tim and me go and see."

"No way," retorted Ina. "I'm the one that's got this," she said, wielding a large piece of wood she'd found on the forest floor. "Anyway, Tim's smaller than me and he doesn't know woods like I know them. He's not one of us," she hissed under her breath.

"Tim?" said Jonnie enquiringly.

"Go on then, someone needs to be here for Evie and Daisy if anything happens. She won't be much good at looking after them," he replied, nodding in Ina's direction.

"Right," nodded Jonnie. "That's settled then, let's go."

Out of the clearing and the light of the pale moon, the forest seemed darker than ever. Even the trees seemed menacing, their branches reaching out to the pair as they pushed through the dense undergrowth.

"Stop," hissed Ina, coming to a halt.

"What is it?" said Jonnie.

"I can feel it," replied Ina.

"Feel what?"

"It's safe, no danger, the danger's passed."

A shiver went all the way from the top of Jonnie's blonde head to the tip of her toes. Her mum had been able to do that. Suddenly she thought of her stuff, back at the van, her crystals and her lace. Ina was right: these people were family, she was one of them, it was in her blood.

"Come on then. Lead on, master." He grinned at her.

Delighted that Jonnie trusted her, Ina crashed through the woods with new confidence, Jonnie close on her tail.

Suddenly Ina gasped, "Oh no," she cried, "We're too late!"

At first glance, Jonnie was inclined to agree: Sid was lying on his side in a pool of water, his legs splayed at odd angles, a chink of moonlight illuminating a bloody gash to the side of his head.

“Dad,” cried Ina, rushing to his side with a sob.

‘Stop, don’t move him,” yelled Jonnie , pushing her to one side. “I’ve seen this before, back at the pit. Last thing you should do is move them, just in case.”

“But we can’t just leave him like that.”

Jonnie lowered her head to Sid’s.”

“Is he?” sobbed Ina.

“No, not dead, just stunned I think. He’s still breathing, at any rate,” replied Jonnie.

“I don’t like the look of that leg, though. I think it’s probably broken in more than one place.”

“We’ve got to get him out of here, who knows who’s around. Once we get back to the vardo Mam will know what to do. She’s good at healing things.”

Suddenly Jonnie remembered something she’d seen done back at the pit.

“Give us your jacket, Ina, then go and get Tim. He’ll help you to fetch a couple of big sticks.”

‘They’re here,” whispered Ina. “I can feel them watching us. What if they attack you and Dad when I’m gone?”

"I can take care of myself and your Dad," replied Jonnie. "Now go: the quicker we get him on a stretcher, the quicker we can be away."

Jonnie quickly scanned the surrounding trees. Although she couldn't see anything, she knew she was right: Geordie and Annie had done this and they weren't too far away. She could almost feel Geordie's hot breath against her cheek.

The forest was very quiet – too quiet. Even the birds seemed to have stopped singing. Sid groaned again.

"Shh," urged Jonnie. "Save your strength for later," she whispered into the injured man's ear.

Sid's eyes opened. "Look to the pool. You have to look to the pool!"

Something about Sid's voice seemed to be changing.

"Look into the darkness, Jonnie. Look into the pool."

Where there had only been one voice before, now there seemed to be a whole host of them, all urging her on.

As if in a trance, she rose and walked slowly towards the pool. Up above her the trees rustled and the forest seemed to close in around her, as if it was protecting her from something. Kneeling down, she looked into the dark waters. At first she could see nothing, just a deep inky blackness that reminded her of the mine.

Then the waters started to clear. Gasping, she spotted Tim and Daisy's mother sitting with a small crowd of women at what looked like the top of the mine shaft. In the background she could see bodies lying on the ground, covered in white sheets. But who was that making their way towards her? As the figure drew closer she drew back in horror: Annie and Geordie's mam; injured but clearly alive, was shouting something to a group of men who looked as if they had been brought in to help with the rescue operation.

"You useless devils! You know you can save them. You heard them! I heard them! I tell you they are still alive."

The men shook their heads. "She ain't right in the head, that one," murmured one under his breath. "She was never right."

"Aye," replied a younger man standing a short distance away from the main group. "But she's right, though. You and me both, we heard them down there crying for help."

"Aye well, that that's as maybe, but neither you nor me are going back down there to find out. Any minute now the whole place could go up."

"So what we going to do then, just leave them down there to die?" retorted the younger man. The older men looked at one another, but before any of them could reply Martha interrupted.

"Aye, and leave another widow and her kids." She gestured towards where Tim's mam was sitting, her toddlers cradled in her arms. "With her main earners gone off and left her she'll be thrown out of her house if her Jay doesn't come back." "Her and her kids."

"So, if ye lot won't shift your behinds, then I will," shouted Martha with a snarl, making for the entrance to the mine.

Gasping in horror, the onlookers watched as the woman they all despised tightened a rope around her waist and, tying it to a nearby tree, disappeared down the mine shaft.

A group of women turned to the men. "Aye well I'd be the first one to admit that I haven't had much time for Martha in the past but at least someone's got guts around here."

"Guts mebbies, but no brains in her head," retorted an older miner. "That mine could collapse at any time and take her with it, and then where would her own bairns be?"

The women laughed. "Reckon little Annie and little Geordie can take care of themselves, wherever they are," replied a big woman dressed in a shawl and long blue apron. The rest of the women nodded in agreement. They all felt the same; up until then none of them would have had a good word to say about Martha, but today they were seeing a different side to her; a side they really liked.

Jonnie drew back from the pool. So Martha was still alive, and there was hope too for Tim and Daisy's dad, and possibly for Bri the banksman too. Relieved, she was just about to turn back to Sid when out of the corner of her eye she saw a flash of light from between the grasses at the edge of the water. Leaning over, she parted the green fronds to reveal a tiny silver wren. As she examined it, Sid gave another groan and hurriedly she pushed it into her pocket and went over to tend to him.

Back at the wagon, with Rosie safely tending to Sid, the trio finally relaxed.

"We have to move on out of here. If they did that to Sid, then they'll come back for us."

"How do you know it was them?" enquired Daisy.

Sid hadn't been able to say a word about how his injury came about, but Jonnie was certain that it must have been Geordie and Annie.

"Can't we sleep first?" replied Tim with a yawn. "I'm dog tired. Surely we'll be all right till morning?"

Beamer barked in agreement.

"You see," grinned Tim. "This lad knows best."

Jonnie shook her head. "No, we have to move now. What Sid said back there makes me think that Geordie and Annie are still around. And if they can do that to Sid, who knows what they'll try and do to Evie and Daisy."

Tim turned pale at the thought of Geordie's stinking breath in his face.

'They must be hungry now too. That'll make them even more dangerous," added Jonnie, grimacing.

In the back of the wagon, Rosie and Daisy tended to Sid.

"Do you think he'll make it?" asked Daisy, handing Rosie a bowl of warm water to wipe Sid's now burning forehead.

'The next few hours will tell," replied Rosie, fighting back tears. "He's a fighter, our Sid. I wouldn't like to be in the shoes of whoever did this to him when he wakes up. I need to get some fresh herbs, to bring down the fever. You'll have to stay here with him while I go to fetch them."

"You can't go out, Ma," said Ina, appearing in the door of the wagon.

"Says who?" demanded Rosie.

"You can't leave him with her," snarled Ina, shaking her head at Daisy.

"You leave her out of it, our Ina. She's a good nurse, is this one. In lots of ways better more fit for it than some around here."

Ina blushed fiercely. The hint wasn't lost on her: she never could stand the sight of blood or be around sickness. Her ma was right; she just wasn't suited to it.

"Jonnie: he says we have to get going and now."

"I have to get these herbs to make Dad better. His fever's going up and up, and at this rate he'll be dead by morning if I don't get them," replied Rosie anxiously, looking back at Sid.

"All right, let's go quickly while Jonnie and Tim make the wagon ready. You keep quiet, or there'll be trouble," hissed Ina turning to Daisy.

'The lads will be looking for you soon. I'll have to tell them where you are, and what about those two that attacked your dad?" demanded Daisy. "You think they'll spare you two?"

Ina furrowed her brow. She would go alone, but she knew that she couldn't be sure to bring back the right herbs, especially in the dark. As Rosie had said, she'd never been very interested in that healing stuff. Not like her ma and other women in her family. She had always preferred to be out with the men, tending to the horses, trapping rabbits and setting snares for wild ducks. She wasn't going to admit that to Daisy though.

"We'll be back before they're ready to go," replied Ina, and with a few last instructions to Daisy she disappeared into the night.

Daisy sat hunched in the back of the wagon, the fading light of a single candle illuminating the sheen of sweat on Sid's face. Rosie had said that his leg was broken and that she would bind it in the morning, but first they had to bring down that fever. She remembered men being brought home from the pit after accidents, terrible accidents. Most of them didn't get better. The women didn't know anything about using herbs and plants to bring down fevers and, even if the men weren't that badly injured, they usually caught infections and died anyway. Outside the window, the dogs began to bark again. In the pale moonlight she could see Tim and Jonnie leading the huge carthorse towards the wagon. Beamer and the three Gypsy dogs were straining to be free, barking and whining at something or someone out of sight in the forest. For the first time since they left Skry, Daisy began to cry. It all seemed so hopeless. All she wanted was to be back with Mam in Skry, back with the little brothers and sisters she left behind. Suddenly a small hand grabbed hers. "Don't cry, Daisy," said Evie, appearing from the bunk above Sid. "It'll be all right, Rosie will make Sid better, then we can go with them. We'll be safe."

Daisy shook her head. "It's all right for you and Jonnie, you don't have anybody back home, but Tim and me; our whole family's back there," replied Daisy, with another sob.

"But we'll be like your family, me and Jonnie," comforted Evie.

Daisy summoned a weak smile. "I suppose you will. You're all we have left now."

"Right," announced Jonnie, entering the wagon. "We're ready for the off. Where's Ina and Rosie?" she demanded.

Daisy and Evie exchanged glances.

'They went out for a bit," replied Daisy.

"Went out! What do you mean, they went out?" yelled Jonnie, her normally pale face flushed with anger.

"They needed some stuff," replied Daisy.

"Stuff, what stuff, what are you talking about, girl? You are not making any sense at all," shouted Jonnie furiously. "They can't go out there with Geordie and Annie around, who knows what'll happen to them."

"We couldn't stop them," cried Daisy. "I tried but Rosie said that she needed the herbs or Sid'll die, and Ina had to go with her."

"Get them!" shouted a voice from outside.

Rushing to the wagon door, Jonnie was just in time to see Rosie and Ina appear from the forest, their hands filled with plants. Behind them she could just make out the furious face of Geordie Giles.

Frantically the pair made for the wagon, stumbling over the uneven ground. They were just about there when Rosie, her hands filled with herbs, stumbled and fell heavily.

"Ma," screamed Ina, dropping her herbs and turning to face Geordie.

Just as Geordie seemed about to close in on them, Tim sprang into action. Grabbing a knife he sawed through the rope leashes that tethered the four dogs.

As the dogs sprang forward Geordie took one look at them, their teeth bared and the whites of their eyes showing, and took off like a shot, back into the forest, the dogs in hot pursuit.

"It's all right, Ma, they've gone now," sobbed Ina, helping Rosie to her feet. "The dogs have seen them off right enough."

"Call them back, girl," whispered Rosie. "We need them for protection. I know them dogs, if they have their way they'll chase that pair all the way back down the pit again."

"I'll get them," said Tim, proud to be able to do something to help.

After what seemed like an age, the four dogs appeared at the edge of the forest, their tongues hanging out. All except for Jet, who looked to have something in his mouth.

"I think Geordie lost a bit of his trousers," grinned Jonnie, wryly.

"Aye, part of his bum too and all," replied Tim delightedly. "He'll not be back in a hurry."

"Right, come on then, let's get going before he changes his mind," said Jonnie. Taking the horse's reins, she gave a gentle tug on her bit. "Come on, Bosher, let's be away from here." The horse gave a gentle whicker and nudged Jonnie with her nose.

"Good with horses and all," nodded Rosie, recovering from her shock. "He really has all of his mother's gifts," she sighed.

"He's going to need them to get us all out of this mess," retorted Ina. "It was a bad day when we said we'd help this lot," she added, with a sniff.

Chapter 16

As the party travelled south, the weather stayed fair and, after a while, the little band fell into a routine. Rosie would tend to Sid by day, applying herb poultices to his broken leg. She and Daisy had fashioned a splint using strong wood from nearby trees, which they bound to his leg with a pair of Ina's old trousers. Rosie also made him a kind of herb tea, which seemed to ease his pain and soothed him enough to get some sleep. Daisy and Tim took turns to drive Bosher the pony, while Ina and Jonnie went out hunting. As the sun started to go down, Rosie and Evie gathered sticks for the campfire, and Rosie would hang her big cooking pot, full of water from a nearby stream, ready for whatever Ina and Jonnie had managed to catch that day. Ina turned out to be a fantastic hunter, catching rabbits, ducks and even the odd pheasant or two. She also taught Jonnie to fish, using a heavy hook, which Sid had made from some old iron, and worms that they dug up (with help from Beamer, Molly, Jet and Jelly). At first Daisy worried about finding fresh water.

"Don't you fret about that," smiled Rosie. "Our Ina's one of the best dowsers in these parts."

"What's a dowser?" enquired Daisy.

"It's where you take a stick shaped like a V, and follow it until it smells water, then it gives a tweak, like this," piped up Evie, moving her arm sharply upwards to show what she meant.

Rosie smiled. "You've been watching Ina at work. Good girl, that's how you learn."

Evie beamed with delight, and Daisy couldn't help but grin. It had been such a relief not to have to look after Evie all on her own. What the girl really wanted was a mum, and Rosie was such a warm cuddly person that she fitted the bill perfectly.

"Here comes dinner," said Rosie, pointing to Jonnie and Ina returning from their hunting trip.

Daisy jumped up to greet them. "What's on tonight then?" she said with a sniff, "Mmm, I bet it's rabbit."

"Aw, not rabbit again," said Tim with an exaggerated sigh. He was a bit fed up of Ina and Jonnie doing all the hunting together. Even when he wanted to join in, Ina wouldn't let him, saying that they needed at least one fit boy at the camp just in case Geordie and Annie showed up again.

He was bored at first, left behind with the women, but after a while, as Sid began to get better, he wanted a man to talk to and would spend hours with Tim, telling him how to handle dogs and horses. He taught Tim how to train the dogs to respond to his whistle, how to fetch a stick, and how to walk to heel even without the string of rope that he'd been using as a leash for Beamer. He also taught him to take care of the horse, making sure that she was brushed, and well fed and watered, ready to travel for the next day. But the best part of the day was when they all sat around the campfire, and Sid and Rosie told tales of the people they'd meet when they finally arrived at the hop fields. Sometimes Daisy would tell her tales about the ghosts of the mine, but they were never quite so vivid or scary. After what they'd been through, the ghost of the Pit Wife didn't seem so terrifying after all. Her tales didn't annoy Tim now; they just made him feel very sad as he wondered what had happened to his mam and the rest of the family, and how they were coping without Dad. Most nights, once the others were sleeping, he would weep, thinking of his dad trapped down the mine, and the terrible fate that had befallen him and his mates. He thought of his mam and Jo, especially of Jo.

"What do you think happened to Jo, then?" asked Rosie one evening.

"I think he just went back to the village," replied Daisy confidently. "Our Jo was never a wanderer, he was never a one for adventure. He'll be back now, taking care of Mam and the rest of them."

"You can't know that," replied Tim worriedly. "Annie and Geordie might have got to him."

"Nonsense," retorted Daisy. "Jo may not be as strong as you but he has twice the brain. He'll be fine."

Jonnie turned away: she couldn't let them know what she had seen; let them know that their dad hadn't been brought up yet but that there was every chance he was alive. Yet, sometimes, like now, she felt guilty for keeping it to herself. Tim was such a worrier, always thinking of what might happen, always anticipating the worst: and the dreams, he and Jonnie's tents were side by side outside the wagon, and Jonnie would often wake to Tim crying out in fear. Yet, when Jonnie went to him, Tim would still be sleeping.

"What's in that bag?" Ina demanded, pointing at the sack by Jonnie's feet.

"You never give up, do you?" she smiled, shaking her head. "I've told you before, what's in that bag is mine and only for me to see."

"Just one little look," persisted Ina. "I won't tell."

Jonnie shook her head. Her mother's things were something she wasn't going to share with anyone at all. Well, perhaps not quite anyone at all. She thought that maybe Rosie might be able to help her to use the crystals. After all, she was Mum's sister and must know something about telling the future. But not yet, not while Sid was still ill. She'd wait a bit, until they arrived at the hop fields, then perhaps she'd ask her advice. Besides, she wasn't sure about Rosie. There was something about the way she sometimes looked at Jonnie that made her think that perhaps Rosie suspected that Jonnie was really Joanna.

Bored now, Ina wandered off to the small stream that ran the length of their camp. Not far now until the hop fields. They were almost in sight of London. Then they could relax a bit more. They'd be safer there with all of their friends around them. Geordie and

Annie wouldn't dare attack them then. Beamer, seeing his friend beside the stream, trotted up to Ina and gave her a wet kiss on the nose.

"Hey old boy, you come to tell me something?" said Ina, patting the dog's smooth coat. Beamer always looked sleek. Even when food was scarce, he always managed to give the appearance of being well fed. Ina stroked his silky ears. "You know what's in that bag, don't you boy?" Beamer looked as if he was grinning. She tickled his ears and he whined with delight. "We'll find out what's in the bag, won't we boy? You and me, eh?" She grinned as the beginning of a plan started to take shape. "Oh yes, Beamer, me boy, you and me, we'll make a grand team."

It was six in the morning when the crew first caught sight of London. Daisy saw it first, rising out of the early morning mist.

"Look," she shrieked. "London ahead!"

"What on earth's got into you, child," scolded Rosie, appearing bleary-eyed from the back of the wagon. "That shouting's enough to wake the dead, not to mention anyone else who wants to know where we are."

Jonnie appeared from behind the wagon, the dogs running at her heels.

"It's London all right," she whispered underneath her breath. "We finally made it."

In the silence of the morning, they could just make out the domes and towers of the capital, shimmering and shining gold in the first morning light.

"It's made of gold," breathed Evie, her eyes wide.

"Like in the books, Jonnie. It's made of gold. Will we be rich there?"

Jonnie smiled. In the early morning light she looked almost as ethereal as the city, her golden hair shining and her blue eyes sparkling with anticipation.

"Well, perhaps not straight away," she replied, "but some day we will be, and at least in London there's a chance for us all, eh, Tim?"

Tim nodded, staring into the middle distance. He wasn't looking at the spires and the towers of the great city: his gaze was drawn by the clouds above them, their fluffy whiteness transforming into shapes that ebbed and flowed with the gentle early morning breeze. As he stared, two of the biggest clouds began to darken and move towards one another and, as they moved, the blue gap between them narrowed until only a sliver of blue appeared between the pair. As the clouds pushed closer and closer together, he could see a shape starting to appear. It looked like a face, and then, just in the split second before the clouds merged into one, he saw her. It was a woman and she was laughing, laughing and pointing at them. And then in a second she was gone.

"Best get on, then," advised Rosie, interrupting their reverie. "We've still a way to go before we get to the hoppings. We have to go through that and out the other side," she added, pointing to the city.

"What's going on, Ma?" shouted Sid from the back of the van. He was much better these days and, with the aid of a crutch that Jonnie and Tim had made him from a dead tree branch, he could get up and about much more easily. They'd tried to get the full story out of him about what had happened that night, but all he could remember was hearing noises in the forest, before something hit him on the back of the head. He couldn't remember seeing Geordie and Annie, though in his half-conscious state he thought he'd heard someone muttering. Occasionally at night the dogs would set to barking again, but whatever was out there never came too close to the wagon again, so their journey passed off fairly peacefully.

"You'll need to keep the dogs close to the wagon as we go through," advised Sid. "The streets of London are dangerous places, lots of loose dogs with no training, and thieves and vagabonds wanting to get their hands on old Bosher here," he added.

"Aye, and Evie, you'll have to stay on the vardo, it's too dangerous for you to be walking the streets," remarked Rosie.

"I'll get ready to loose the dogs on anybody that gets too close," said Tim.

"Yes, and I'll be ready with this," said Ina, brandishing her baton with a grin.

"Doesn't sound like a very nice place, from what you are saying," questioned Jonnie.

'That's right, too many thieves and beggars, all wanting to get something from you. And disease as well. It's a dirty filthy place, they've got the sickness there, so don't let anyone touch you," said Rosie.

"What sickness?" asked Daisy.

"All manner of sicknesses," replied Ina darkly. "You'll see when we get there."

"Jonnie, even you'll have to sleep in the vardo once we arrive," said Rosie looking away.

"Mmmm, we'll see," said Jonnie, glad that Rosie couldn't see the anxious look in her eyes. How much longer could she keep her secret? Especially if she had to undress in front of Rosie.

The children spent the rest of the journey in silence that day, each lost in thought about what horrors awaited them in London. They were so busy with their thoughts that they didn't catch sight of the two ragged figures peering at them from the bushes.

Annie and Geordie had not had such an easy journey. No rest on the wagon for them. They had made the whole journey from Skry to London on foot, sleeping in hayricks and ditches at night. Unaccustomed to living life on the road, they had found very little food and relied instead on scraps they managed to steal from the odd farm or other traveller. Geordie had not had any treatment for the nasty bite inflicted on him by the Gypsy dog and, left to fester, the wound had become infected and ulcerated, leaving him with a permanent limp. His temper was even worse than before. Although he didn't like any of them, his hatred was mainly aimed at Jonnie and Tim, and he seethed and planned what he would do once he had the opportunity.

"We have to get rid of the dogs before we make our move. Those things have to die."

Annie nodded. "Poison will do it, and we can get poison once we're down in London. Then all we need to do is put it somewhere

where those stupid animals will eat it. Whatever that Gypsy's got in that bag will be ours then. Chances are it's something valuable, the way it never leaves his side, eh?"

Geordie nodded, his eyes narrowing as he caught sight of Jonnie driving the wagon.

"What'll really get him the most is if we take the kid though," he added, staring over at Evie who was happily running alongside the wagon, oblivious to the danger that lurked so close.

Annie nodded. "What would we do with her though? Just another mouth to feed."

"Mmm, I'll think of something. Plenty down in the city that would pay for a good servant girl," he sniggered.

Annie wasn't so sure. She never openly dared to disagree with her big brother but, as her mam had often said, Geordie wasn't the brightest spark in the fire: he would often say things that seemed silly to her. And lately, since they'd left Skry – she didn't know if it was his leg or just the hatred he felt for Jonnie and Tim – he seemed to be getting angrier and angrier and less able to see things as they really were. Time after time he'd done things that didn't seem to make any sense. Like hitting out at Jo: why bother? The lad was only making his way home, why try to kill him? And hitting that Gypsy man, what was the sense in that? It had only made the party more wary that they might be attacked, and stopped any chance that Geordie and Annie might have had at sneaking up on them unawares.

Then there was the food issue. Annie had wanted to beg for food – far safer – but Geordie had insisted that begging was a mug's game. He had preferred to steal, and now people would be after them, especially after what had happened a couple of days back. Annie shuddered when she thought of that. They had been starving as usual and Geordie's temper was up, especially as Jonnie and the Gypsy girl seemed to be so good at being able to hunt and fish, where Geordie was completely useless. They'd arrived at a small croft well off the beaten track and, after watching it for a couple of hours, they decided it looked to be inhabited by just one woman and her young son and daughter. Either there was no father, or he was away. Annie had begged Geordie to let her approach the lady, who had a kind face: she was sure that in her ragged state she'd be able to beg some bread and, if she was lucky, perhaps some milk as well.

"All right, we'll do it your way," Geordie growled. "But if it doesn't work then we do it my way."

Annie nodded and knocked on the door of the croft.

"Please, ma'am, can you give me something to eat? I'm starving after my mam and dad died and left me all alone in the world."

The woman took one look at the ragged creature standing on her doorstep and immediately took pity on the poor thing.

"You come indoors here, and we'll see what we can do for you." Her own husband had gone away to fight some time ago, and had sadly never returned. She knew how hard it was to survive without a man's wages, so to hear this sad creature's tale broke her heart.

“My two will be in shortly and I’m making a meal for them, so a bit extra won’t hurt.”

Annie stared at the woman, taken aback. She hadn’t expected to be invited in for a meal. The best she’d hoped for was something that she could take back to Geordie and share; although she knew that Geordie rarely shared anything and all too often she went hungry, while he gorged himself on whatever he had managed to steal.

“Come here, I might have something that my daughter has grown out of. Those clothes can’t keep you very warm at night.” The woman nodded at Annie’s torn and ragged trousers and jacket.

Following the woman upstairs – she told Annie she was called Jess – Annie gasped in wonder as they entered the small but beautifully furnished bedroom: the patchwork quilts a riot of bright colours, the walls decorated with sketches of animals and plants.

‘That’s our Mary’s work,” said Jess, noticing the wondering look on Annie’s face.

“She’s a real artist. Ben is too, but he works in wood. Look, here are some of his carvings.”

Annie picked up a tiny, intricate carving from the dresser.

"That one took him ages. He went out studying the sheep and their lambs for days, so that he could get the detail just right. Look, even the tiny lambs' tails are perfect," added Jess.

"Here this will do you," she said, holding up a clean white smock and underskirt.

"I don't wear dresses," growled Annie, suddenly remembering why she was there.

"Oh, and you'd look so pretty in one. If we just cleaned you up a bit, you'd look a treat," smiled Jess, ignoring the girl's surly tone.

For a second, Annie was tempted. Her clothes were so badly torn and no protection at all against the weather. Then she thought of her mother. She tried not to think of her mam much these days. Oh, she'd been a bad mum all right but, at the end of the day, she was still the only mam she had, and she missed her. Martha had never been one for dresses.

"You keep your trousers on girl, even after work. That way you'll never get no bother," said Martha often enough. Annie had never seen her mam in a dress, although she did once see a picture. One rare day when Martha was out, and Annie was trying to make the cold smelly hovel where they lived a bit more comfortable, she found it under the bed. It was a sketch. She recognised her mam's face straight away, but it was so much prettier than the mam she knew: the clothes weren't grand, but she'd never forgotten that picture of her mam in the simple white dress; a beautiful Martha, a smiling Martha. Then, one night shortly after, her mam had come in drunk. Even Geordie stayed out of the way when she came in in one of her moods. At first she stormed into the room she called a bedroom, even though it was just a mattress on the bare floor, and as Annie peered through a crack in the door she saw her mam scrabbling under the mattress, throwing things around the room. As Annie looked out of the window, she spotted her mother hurling something into the fire. As she watched she realised that it was the little sketch. Horrified, she made for the fire. Drawing level with her mam, she was just about to plunge her hand into the fire to retrieve it when Martha turned to her. Annie stopped still. There were tears running down her mother's face, the first tears that she had ever seen her mam shed.

"Leave it lass, it's gone now," said Martha.

The pair stood in silence together, watching as the bright flames died black and the cold dawn shone grey over the horizon.

Then Martha turned to Annie. "Never trust, girl. Never trust anyone. That was my downfall, I trusted and I lost. Don't let it ever happen to you."

Annie nodded at her mother. This was the most her mam had ever really said to her, and the strange thing was, she wasn't shouting or teasing like normal.

"Yes, Mam, I'll remember."

That was the last and only time that Martha seemed to treat Annie like the daughter she was. After that, things went back to normal: Martha getting drunk, screaming, swearing and hitting out at them at night; and in the day just long hours of back-breaking work in the dark.

Sensing the girl's dilemma, Jess thought hard. The girl looked to be dressed like a boy, but that was quite common for beggar girls. They attracted less attention to themselves that way, a good thing when you were travelling alone. "What about a pair of Ben's old trousers then? They would see you nice and warm," she suggested, handing Annie a pair of thick woollen culottes.

Begrudgingly, Annie took them. "I'll leave you to it then, there's a jug and basin there for you to have a bit of a wash up. Just come down when you're ready," added Jess, leaving Annie alone.

Alone in the room, Annie sighed as she caught sight of herself in the mirror. Her face still bore the signs of pit dust, now overlaid with the dirt and dust of the road. Her hair, matted and tangled, gave her a wild look like one of the lunatics in the asylum that her mam had been in when her drinking got out of hand. Tentatively, she raised the porcelain jug and poured a little water into the creamy blue and white basin.

'That's better," beamed Jess, when Annie at last reappeared downstairs. "You look like a girl again now!"

Annie nodded at the woman, unsmilingly. It was so long since she'd had anything to really smile about that she'd almost forgotten how. Smirking, yes; smirking came naturally to her, but smiling?

"Ah, here we are," said Jess, as a tall curly-haired lad entered the room. "This is Ben, and this is my daughter, Mary."

Ben was tall, almost as tall as Geordie, but far better-looking, with dark curly hair and a ready smile.

"Pleased to meet you," he said, coming forward and taking her hand.

Annie backed away. No one had ever tried to shake hands with her before.

"What's your name?" asked Mary gently.

"Mavis," mumbled Annie.

"Mavis, that's a lovely name. We've a lamb called Mavis, isn't that right, Ben?"

‘That’s right. Reckon you’d like to see her after tea? We’re feeding her ourselves. Her mum died when she was born, so we’ve been giving her milk from a bottle.”

Annie nodded.

“Come on then, tea’s ready,” said Jess. “Plenty of time for talk after we’ve eaten.”

No sooner had Jess set down a steaming plate of stew in front of the girl than Annie began to wolf it down. She was so ravenous, she didn’t even notice as Ben and Mary exchanged horrified glances: they had never seen anyone eat like that before. Annie’s spoon lay shining clean as she plunged her hands into the hot stew and licked it noisily off her fingers. Unseen by all of them, Geordie’s filthy face peered in through the window.

He watched them for a while, his hot breath steaming up the window, before disappearing.

It was dark by the time the children reached the barn.

“You’ll need to be quiet here,” ordered Ben, as the three of them crept by stalls filled with a variety of animals: from a lovely brown cow named Bluebell, to a couple of goats called Jock and Andy. By the time they reached the stall where Mavis lived, Annie was almost smiling. She had never felt like this before: her belly full and the warmth and friendship of Mary and Ben, the kind of friendship she had never known back in Skry.

But, as Ben rounded the corner, his candle outstretched, Mary and Annie suddenly heard him gasp.

“No, Mavis, not my Mavis,” he cried.

For when he raised his candle, the young lamb, illuminated by the dim light, was lying cold and stiff on her side in the stall.

Choking back sobs, Mary rushed from the barn, followed by a horrified Annie. Annie had seen many dead animals in her time so she wasn’t really shocked by the sight of Mavis, but Mary’s crying had really upset her.

As the pair reached the house, Mary dashed in through the front door. Annie was just about to follow when she felt a heavy hand on her shoulder, dragging her back.

“Come on, you, you’ve lived the high life now, eh? Had a taste of it in them fancy pants and your belly full, where mine is rumbling away.”

“Geordie,” cried Annie in horror. “I have to go, Geordie, I have to be with Mary now.”

“You ain’t going nowhere, Miss Fancy Pants, you’re coming with me to do what we set out to do.”

"No Geordie," screamed Annie. "I can't do this any more!" she cried, sobbing.

"Ah, I see, my precious, one day with posh folk and you forget about your brother, forget your mam and her killers," he screamed in her face.

Suddenly, through the darkness, Ben appeared white-faced from the stable. Spotting Annie and Geordie in the yard, he stopped short, hiding behind a large bale of hay.

"On the road then, my duck, off we go," shouted Geordie, hauling Annie up by her hair.

Ben hung back, his eyes following Annie as, with shoulders hunched, she pulled herself up and trailed after the boy that seemed to be her brother.

He watched them until they disappeared, their footsteps illuminated by the pale moonlight, before he went inside to break the sad news to his mum.

Chapter 17

It was daybreak when the wagon reached the outskirts of London town and they stopped for a well-earned rest on a hill.

"You can see the whole of London from here," said Sid, now doing quite well on his crutches.

Jonnie stared at the scene before them. What a huge place London was, spread out like that, its river glistening like a snake in the distance.

"I'm scared," said Evie, sucking her thumb.

"What for, my lamb?" replied Rosie, giving her a hug. "No place is dangerous if we are with you: your Auntie Rosie and Uncle Sid will look out for you, you know that."

Evie smiled and returned the hug.

"Well Tim, what do you make of it?" asked Jonnie.

"It looks like I thought it would," replied Tim.

"Have we got to get all of the way across that?" cried Daisy, aghast.

"Yes," nodded Ina, smugly. "Tough week it'll be getting through that lot, before we get to the hoppings."

For a moment the crew were silent, then Jonnie spoke.

"Well, we've got this far. A bit further won't hurt, eh?"

"You mean, you can put up with us for a bit longer then?" grinned Ina.

"Mmm, well, maybe just a bit," grinned Jonnie, digging Tim in the ribs.

Beamer gave a little whimper, but no one really noticed. They were too busy looking at the big city and thinking of crossing it safely, of the fun waiting for them when they finally reached the hoppings.

But Beamer's gaze had fallen on the pair that lay unseen, crouched in the bushes, the boy with the big stick that had hurt Sid.

Jonnie stared into the distance, her fingers closing around the silver wren she had picked up from the forest floor. Drawing it from her pocket she held it in the air, its upturned tail catching the early morning sun. Smiling, she replaced it safely in her pocket.

"Come on then, everyone, what are we waiting for? We don't want to be late for the hoppings now, do we? To London! Quick march!"

The End

Research Bibliography

Anderson, M. (2009). *Northumberland and Cumberland Mining Disasters*. Barnsley,South Yorkshire: Wharncliffe Books

Armstrong, K., & Dixon, P. (2012). *Still the Sea Rolls on: The Hartley Pit Calamity of 1862*. Whitley Bay: Northern Voices Community Projects in association with North Tyneside Council.

Bell, D. (2006). *Derbyshire Coalfields*. Newbury: Countryside Books Evans, S. (2004). *Stopping Places: A Gypsy history of South London and Kent* Hatfield: University of Hertfordshire Press.

Forster, E. (1978). *The Pit Children*. Durham: Frank Graham: Newcastle on Tyne.

Gallop, A. (2003). *Children of the Dark:Life and death underground in Victoria's England*. Stroud: Sutton Publishing Ltd.

Griffiths, B. (2007). *Pitmatic: The Talk of the North East Coalfield*. Newcastle Upon Tyne: Northumbria University Press.

John, A. (1984a). *By the Sweat of their brow: women workers at Victorian coal mines*. London: Routledge and Kegan Paul.

John, A. (1984b). *Coalmining Women: Victorian Lives and Campaigns*. Cambridge Cambridge University Press.

Kenrick, D., & Puxon, G. (1972). *The Destiny of Europe's Gypsies*. London: Sussex University Press in association with Heinemann Educational Books

Lake, F., & Preece, R. (1992). *Voices from the Dark: Women and Children in Yorkshire Coal Mines* Overton: Yorkshire Mining Museum Publications.

Lee, R. (2005). *Learn Romani : Das-Duma Rromanes*. Hatfield: University of Hertfordshire Press.